# The Bohemian Connection

**A novel**

**by**

**Tom Creary**

**ISBN: 978-0-9921520-0-0**

To Diane, Ben, Simon and my Bohemian ancestors


With a special thanks to Michèle Thienel
in making this a readable story

# Preface

The story in this book is fiction. Nevertheless, the places mentioned exist and most of the historical incidents described actually occurred, although some have been expanded upon and fictionalized. The characters in the novel are fictional, although some have been based on people I have known.

Tom Creary, June 2013

# Cast of characters

Erik Brandt - retired German diplomat, head of Brandt family

Isabel Brandt - wife of Erik Brandt

Georg, Richard, Karl and Claudia Brandt, children of Erik and Isabel Brandt

Lucas Brandt - son of Georg Brandt and grandson of Erik Brandt

Elizabeth Black Brandt - mother of Lucas

Ingrid Waller - Viennese friend of Isabel

Michael Coburg (originally Michael Cobourg-Strauss) - Viennese stage actor

Karl Cobourg-Strauss, Austrian philanthropist, uncle of Michael Coburg

Vilem Slavata - Bohemian nobleman, owner of Jindrichuv Hradec Castle and Chancellor of Bohemia (1620-1632)

Anthony Wong - Singapore criminal lawyer

Stanley He - former diplomat, advisor to Government of Singapore

André Gralla - French businessman, husband of Claudia Brandt

Marco and Luca Scalia - Italian businessmen, cousins of André Gralla

Antonia Scalia, wife of Marco Scalia

Maurice and Hanna Gralla - Czech grandparents of André Gralla

Caroline Weber - American woman, descendant of Bohemian family that emigrated to the United States

Thomas Weber - great-great-grandfather of Caroline Weber

Raymond Weber, Kansas farmer, great-grandson of Thomas Weber, father of Caroline

Barbara Strauss Weber - wife of Thomas, member of Cobourg-Strauss family of Bohemia and Austria

Father Frank Kurtz, parish priest, Wamego, Kansas

Clarence Seitz, caretaker of St. Joseph's Catholic Church, Flush, Kansas

Charles Schreiber, retired Kansas farmer, friend of Weber family

Bonnie Williams, Registrar of Deeds, Pottawatomie County, Kansas

Giuseppe Orini, cobbler, Isola del Giglio, Italy, friend of Erik Brandt

# Chapter 1

## Singapore, April, 1999

"Mr. Brandt, you are under arrest for the importation of drugs" said the airport police officer. "The penalty for importing heroin in this country is life imprisonment or death. I advise you to seek legal help. You will need it."

"What?! There must be some mistake. I have nothing to do with the traffic of drugs," said the young man. "I am an economist with the World Bank in Washington. I was in Jakarta doing a feasibility study for an industrial complex. I discussed marketing agreements with a variety of Indonesian business interests. This cannot be!"

"We found this in the kilo-sized bag of coffee you had in your luggage," replied the official, showing a small transparent plastic bag in his hand.

"That bag of coffee was given to me by my hosts in Jakarta as they drove me to the airport. I had no idea anything else could be inside. I am innocent!"

# Chapter 2

**Heidelberg, Germany, November 1937**

Erik Bendt was concerned. His twin brother, Helmut, had joined the Nazi Party four years before and was becoming an increasingly visible and vocal party official. Helmut's anti-Semitism was particularly distressing.

The brothers had grown up in Munich after the Great War, following their father, Richard von Bendt, who had been one of the Kaiser's diplomats in Asia. After the defeat of Germany, Herr von Bendt had been excluded from further service by the Socialists who had taken control of the government. Von Bendt had inherited a good deal of money and a number of properties in southern Germany, Italy and the south of France from his mother. He had managed to maintain the upkeep of the properties as Germany careened from post-war troubles to economic despair through the twenties to the rise of the National Socialist Party in the early 1930's. After his wife died in a car accident in 1926 and with Hitler's accession to power in 1932, Herr von Bendt

10

uprooted himself from Munich. He now lived alone in one of his possessions on an island in the Tyrrhenian Sea off the west coast of Italy.

Erik's best friend at Heidelberg University was Karl Cobourg-Strauss, from a distinguished family of Austrians who owned a large estate in Czechoslovakia. Karl's father was one of the leading experts in Europe on Judaism and anti-Semitism and his ideas on the subject had a profound effect on his son. Karl's influence on the subject had molded much of what Erik had come to view regarding the Jewish people in Europe. In Erik's mind, the hate expressed towards the Jews and their persecution by the Nazis were destroying the integrity and worthiness of Germans as a modern, tolerant, progressive people.

"Father, I can't live with this here. Helmut has become one of the leading Nazis in the city and I, as a Bendt, am being painted with the same brush by many of my colleagues and friends who are not followers of Herr Hitler, however well they may know me. I am not proud of our name right now."

"I have become as distressed as you with the direction of your brother's life," replied his father.

"Well, Father, Helmut and I have grown apart. I don't even want to be seen with him. I have decided to leave Germany at the conclusion of my studies this year. I do not like what is going on. Mother was Swiss. I should be able to go there."

"Do what you must, Erik. I can't disagree with you. Going to Switzerland would be wise. You already have Swiss citizenship through your mother. Her extensive family is well established and will be able to help you. I will help you as well. You know that. Europe is in distress. Germany is being driven by hate by this so-called Fuhrer. Keep me informed of your plans."

---

Richard von Bendt died of a stroke in January 1938. A few months later, Erik Horst Bendt changed his name to Erik Brandt, taking his mother Hilda's family name. In October 1938, Herr Brandt began his tenure as an instructor in European history at the Interlaken Kantonschule for Boys.

# Chapter 3

## Prague, May 23, 1618

Count Slavata was thrown out the window of the Great Hall of Hradcany Castle along with another Catholic nobleman and the Secretary of the local regent. They landed on a pile of garbage three stories below which saved their lives. This incident became known in History as the Second Defenestration of Prague.

The Protestant nobles had come to Prague to confront the representatives of the Catholic Habsburg Emperor Ferdinand. They were demanding the Emperor's respect of their right to practice their religion and protested the closing of two of their churches. Slavata and his companions dismissed their demands and ordered them out of the room. They instead were the ones who left the room, by the window. This seemingly minor event triggered the bloody Thirty Years War of Europe.

Vilem Slavata was injured but rescued from the refuse pile by members of the crowd loyal to the monarchy who managed to get him beyond the castle gates and out of the city. He made it back to Jindrichuv Hradec, the seat of the Slavata family domain. The castle there was considered the third largest and one of the most celebrated of Bohemia. It was named after Slavata's wife's family. Fifty years before, the scion of the Hradec family, Adam I, had been named one of the eight richest men in Bohemia. His son Adam II managed, within twenty years of taking over, to lose practically the entire family fortune through gambling and unwise commercial ventures. His strong-willed wife, Catherine de Montfort, took over the domain's estates and saved what remained. The Hradec line ended in 1604 with the deaths of Adam II and Catherine. A few years before, their eldest daughter had married Vilem Slavata, a merchant's son, who became master of the Hradec domains.

In recognition of his loyalty and the near sacrifice of his life, Vilem Slavata was made Chancellor of Bohemia by Emperor Ferdinand. In his own gesture of gratitude, Slavata ceded to Maximilian Trauttdorf, his principal rescuer at Prague, the domain of Ronsperg in Western Bohemia., where he built a castle. In 1623, Herr Trauttdorf married Vilem's daughter. In 1626 he was made a Count and became one of the Emperor's most trusted envoys to the courts of Europe.

# Chapter 4

**Westmoreland, Kansas, June 1999**

On a sultry day in the heat of a Kansas summer, the young blond woman entered the Pottawatomie County records office in the small town of Westmoreland. Caroline Weber had grown up on a large farm a few miles from Westmoreland. She had attended the University of Kansas, where she had graduated that spring with a degree in history and political science. Months before, she had decided to pursue some long overdue research on what little she knew of the origins of her family before beginning work in the fall with a Kansas City-based research foundation.

Caroline had been told in her childhood that the family's ancestors on her father's side had emigrated from Vienna in the 1870's and had bought land not far from the small village of Flush. The village didn't exist anymore. All that was left was St. Joseph's Catholic church (or Kirche as it read in stone above the church's heavy double wooden doors), built in 1892 to serve the descendants of Bohemian settlers who came to the area in the preceding decades. The church had been essentially closed since the late 1970's, except for special Christmas and Easter Masses.

Little of the family's history had passed down to Caroline. Her paternal grandparents had both died when she was a young girl and her father was an only child. He had never demonstrated much interest in the origins of the Webers. So Caroline was virtually starting from scratch in her search. Through an ancestry web site, she had discovered in the U.S. Census of 1900 that Thomas Weber, her great-great-grandfather, supposedly from Vienna, Austria, had lived on a plot of land on Noel Road six miles west of Westmoreland. He lived there alone and had declared that he had been born in Bohemia (not Austria) in 1828. Caroline discovered she was of Bohemian ancestry, not Austrian, as her family had always believed.

Her objective that day was to discover exactly where the original family land had been, who her great-great-grandfather had bought it from, when, and how it had been disposed of.

What she discovered shocked her. Her ancestor owned far more than the 160 acre section of land along Noel Road where he lived in 1900. Bonnie Williams, the Pottawatomie county registrar of deeds, showed Caroline that Thomas Weber had bought seven properties in the County from the Union Pacific Railway in 1874. Mrs. Williams also showed her references to other transactions that Mr. Weber had concluded in nearby counties. Armed with the contact information for the records offices in the counties to the east and west of Westmoreland, within two weeks Caroline had discovered that Thomas Weber had bought from the railway and other large landholders in the 1870's parcels of land totaling fourteen thousand acres. The purchases were in an area stretching from Leavenworth on the banks of the Missouri River in the east to the area around what is now Junction City, 40 miles further west of Westmoreland. Fourteen thousand acres! Thomas Weber had apparently been a rich man before even arriving in America.

Just as the recorded purchases were revealing to Caroline, so were the records of disposal of them. In each records office where the Weber transactions had been logged, Caroline was provided evidence of her great-great-grandfather's seemingly random and wholesale disposal of sections of his landholdings during the 1890's. The last remaining plot of land of 160 acres where Thomas had lived was auctioned off to pay off a large debt five years after his death in 1906, and had changed hands a number of times since then. No wonder, Caroline thought, there were no records of any of this in her family. They were undoubtedly shamed or disgusted or both and were certainly relatively impoverished through what appeared to be the squandering of the family wealth by the old man.

What had happened to the proceeds of the sale of over fourteen thousand acres in the boom times of frontier Kansas and, as well, how did Thomas Weber acquire his wealth in the first place? The answer to the first question was probably lost to her forever, for there were no family members around who knew any of this. The answer to the second could be easier to find. Perhaps in Vienna, but more likely in Bohemia in the present Czech Republic.

Caroline was also informed by the registrar that many records of the Austrian and Bohemian Catholic community of the area were kept in the old St. Joseph's Church rectory. The last parish priest, the elderly Father Biehler, had died sometime in the 1970's and no one had replaced him. Flush didn't even exist anymore. She added that the keys to the old rectory building were kept by an old man. No one seemed to know where he lived anymore, but he had been seen from time to time over the years entering the old building. She told Caroline that her brother-in-law cuts the grass around the church and in the cemetery across the road, under a longstanding agreement with the Wamego Catholic parish office. "They never miss a payment," she added.

The next day Caroline made plans to travel in August to the Czech Republic with a stopover in Vienna.

# Chapter 5

## Vienna, June 1967

Isabel Brandt entered the Burgtheatre with Ingrid, her long-time childhood friend. They were both looking forward to the play. Isabel, at 43, was a very attractive woman – tall, slim, elegant, with long sandy blond hair. She had always been a lover of theatre, of music and poetry, and loved Vienna. With the boys away at school and her husband on another mission abroad, she decided to spend a week in the old Imperial capital for a holiday where she could indulge her passion for theatre, music and the genteel cafe life of the city.

Isabel had not seen Ingrid Waller for a long time. It had been years. Her great friend from schooldays had immediately said yes to the proposal to spend some time together and catch up on the course of their lives. They decided to spend Isabel's first evening in Vienna by attending the play at the classic Burgtheatre in the old city center and, of course, find a table later at one of the elegant cafes nearby.

Isabel had a recent history of mild depression and spent a lot of time alone. Her husband, Erik Brandt, was often absent, travelling extensively as the senior diplomatic representative of the German government for European affairs. He had decided the year before to put their three boys into boarding school. It had been over Isabel's objections.

Michael Coburg was 29 and had earned a reputation in the Vienna theatre-going public as a new, exciting leading man. It was the fortieth or so showing of the play. He loved the part, one of a personable, yet devious and unscrupulous scamp. The reviews had been good.

The blond woman sitting in the fourth row next to a lady he knew as Ingrid was stunning. Michael had trouble concentrating. His eyes kept coming back to her. Such a beautiful face, but how melancholic she seemed to be. Their eyes kept meeting.

The Cafe Griensteidl, not far away from the theatre on Michaelerplatz, was packed. Playgoers went there, joining people who had earlier stopped by on the way home from work. As soon as the young actor entered the baroque-styled old café, he saw the woman from the fourth row, sitting at a table in earnest conversation with Ingrid. Wearing a form fitting silk cream-colored blouse with a striking mauve scarf around her shoulders, overlaid with her beautiful long, curly blond hair, she was every bit as attractive a woman as he had ever seen. He had to meet her.

"Hello, Ingrid. You may remember me from the party at the Trestle a few weeks ago. I saw you in the crowd tonight."

"Why, yes, hello, Michael. I do remember and yes, we were there tonight. How are you?"

"I am very well. Did you enjoy the play?"

"Yes, I did enjoy it. You are very good in that role; however, I must say that you are not totally credible as a cheat! Michael, I must introduce you to Isabel, a childhood friend who now lives in France but is here in Vienna for a few days. She was at the theatre with me tonight."

"Yes, I know. I saw you both. In the fourth row, I believe. Enchanté, Madame."

Isabel, shyly, but with a smile, replied "Enchanté. I enjoyed the play as well."

Ingrid motioned to a vacant chair. "You seem to be alone here tonight. Would you like to join us? We have ordered some coffee and pastries. Isabel has been dying to have an Apple Strudel."

Michael sat down and lost himself in the gaze of the beautiful, quiet woman he had just been introduced to.

---

"I am enchanted with you. I can't get you out of my mind. You are lovely, you are divine, your eyes burn into mine, and I am helpless. These last three days and nights have been so sweet and wonderful and so intense. I want to devour you."

Isabel was propped on her elbow next to Michael in the bed as he spoke and replied while caressing his shoulder, inches from her. "When you invited me to see you once again, I had no idea it would come to this. I have never had an affair before. And I have never thought that I could possibly have one with someone so much younger than I. I have not told you much about my life, other than I do have a husband and I will feel guilty, I know. But right now, I don't. You have devoured me, I'm afraid, Michael. I am all yours. I don't want this to end."

"I don't either. I will follow you to Provence. We will not be playing in August. I will go to see you. I don't know what else I can say. I love your words. I love your mind and I admit, I love every inch of you."

---

Three evenings later, Isabel and Michael were again at the Cafe. Isabel had seen his play three times by then. Ingrid happened to be there on her way home from a late stay at work. Soon after warm greetings amongst the three, Michael went off to greet a friend who had hailed him from the bar. Ingrid leaned over to Isabel.

"My dear, you have really gone for him, haven't you? Why are you doing this? I haven't seen you since Tuesday. I thought Erik and you were solid. I'm really surprised, but maybe I shouldn't be."

"Ingrid, I have not been happy. I am alone most of the time now. The boys are gone. Erik is increasingly not around. When he is, it takes us days to re-connect and then he is gone again – to London, Brussels, New York, wherever. We have sex so infrequently now, that when we do, it's like I'm with a stranger. He thinks I'm having a fine time in Provence. But I am not. I have been extremely lonely and I realize now I was vulnerable when I got here. But right now, I don't care what drove me to this. I am just doing it, enjoying every minute of it."

Isabel continued. "Michael has been sweet, gentle, considerate, listening, passionate – all of that. I guess I have just needed somebody to show me some affection and Michael has done that – he has become a light in my life. If it's an affair, it's a real one, I'm afraid. I can't get enough of him. He is coming to Provence towards the end of August. I will find a way to be with him. Hopefully, Erik will be taking the boys somewhere and I will be able to see Michael all I want."

"It has been magic and it started at that table right over there. I guess you can say this grand place has become our own special Viennese Café!"


**Three weeks later....**

The telephone rang in the villa on the edge of St-Rémy de Provence. Isabel answered as she was finishing her early morning coffee. The call was from Ingrid and, for Isabel, surprisingly early for a phone call from her friend in Vienna.

"Isabel, I have terrible news for you. Brace yourself, my dear. Michael was killed in a car accident yesterday. I'm so sorry.

It was on the news here last night." Ingrid continued to speak ...
"a car coming the other way apparently crossed into his
lane.....they said he was killed instantly...." but Isabel was no
longer hearing. She put the phone down on the table and slowly
began to cry.

---

A month after the phone call, Isabel and Erik were seated
across from each other on the terrace of the villa.

"Erik, I have something to tell you. I am pregnant.... You
are not the father." After a brief pause, she continued, "I had an
affair with a young man in Vienna. I am sorry. You must know
that the young man is dead. He was killed in a car accident q
month ago. The affair was an affair. He is gone now, but the child
is real and I intend to bear it."    Isabel raised her head,
straightened her back, looked straight into the eyes of her
husband, and with a solemn face, braced herself for the reaction.

Erik Brandt, aware over the years of his wife's increasing
loneliness and unhappiness as he moved about in his world that
he could not give up, absorbed what she was telling him. Shaken,
and silent for a moment, he asked in a faint voice "Who is he? Or
rather, who was he? I guess it would be right for me to know the
identity of the father of my wife's child."

"His name is Michael Coburg, a stage actor I met while in
Vienna."

"My God, Isabel, has it come to this?" said a stunned Erik. He looked into his wife's eyes, to a face stoic with resolve but clearly holding back tears which he knew would soon come.

He took a deep breath, looked off into the trees at the back of the garden, then dropped his head. After a long moment of silence, with neither saying a word, he muttered "Michael Coburg...Michael Coburg...actor." After another moment of silence, he continued, keeping his gaze on the trees, "My old friend from university, Karl, Karl Cobourg-Strauss, told me a couple of years ago that he had a nephew who had become an actor in Vienna. The young man had turned his back on the family business, and had apparently changed his name to suit the stage." He turned to his wife, now with tears slowly rolling down her cheeks, "I think this Michael Coburg could be the nephew of Karl. This could very well be. Why, Isabel, why?" he implored as he gazed into his wife's eyes across the large table. "Have we grown so far apart? I can't believe what you are telling me."

"I am sorry, Erik, but I was vulnerable," choking on her words as the tears rolled down her face. "You won't like me to say this, but you have neglected me. You are never here. The intensity of our early years is no more and hasn't been there for some time. I got swept off my feet by an engaging man years younger than I. But it happened, and now I am with his child. I should have been more careful, that is for sure, but it happened."

After a short pause, she continued, "Divorce me, whatever. I am sorry, but then, I am not sorry so much in regards to you. I am being frank with you, Erik. I am sorry for me. That young man showed me a love and affection that you have not shown me for years. I don't think that can ever come back."

After a few moments of silence, looking at Isabel in a gaze of sadness and bewilderment, Erik Brandt, the rational career diplomat, accustomed to being in command of everything around him, was in pain and uttered in a low and faltering voice "This will be difficult to live through, Isabel. I don't want a divorce. The boys would be devastated." After a pause, Erik continued. "As to the pregnancy, you could abort the child. It would make everything so much simpler. I could try to make it up to you. I will do all I can for that."

After another moment's silence, Erik asked of his wife "Who else knows about this?"

"No one. I saw a doctor in a clinic in Toulouse and did not give my real name."

"Did the young man know you were pregnant?"

"No, Erik. I told you. He was killed in an accident and it happened before I even learned I was pregnant. Only you and I know, plus a doctor many kilometers from here who I paid cash for the examination who doesn't know my real name."

"It would be simple with an abortion. We could go to Stockholm for it. No one here would know."

"No, Erik. I am a Bavarian Catholic. You know that. An abortion is out of the question. I will have the child. I am sorry....You can do what you want." With that, she turned and went to her bedroom.

Erik walked out to the garden in the twilight of the late evening. I can't have people knowing my wife is having a child from another man, he thought. No. I will not have it that way. And I can't afford to go through a divorce. I don't want to be unmarried to Isabel, in any case. I have neglected her, but I don't want to leave her. I will consider the child as my own. The parents for the record will be Erik and Isabel Brandt. I will simply have to live with the news of this, however distasteful it is. I will ask Isabel to bury this secret and for everyone, we will simply be having another child, albeit rather late after the others. Oh, Isabel, how I have failed you so, he murmured, for only himself to hear.

**France-Soir, 3 août, 1967**

**Décès du comédien de théâtre Michael Coburg, 29 ans, à Graz, Autriche, le 15 juillet, 1967. Né Michael Cobourg-Strauss à Pilsen (Plzen), Czechoslovakie, le 14 mars, 1938. Fils des défunts Richard et Greta Cobourg-Strauss de Ronsperg (Pobezovice), Czechoslovakie et de Vienne. Neveu de Karl Cobourg-Strauss, historien et philanthrope Autrichien.....**

## Diary entry:  St-Remy, August 12, 1967

I am going to have Michael's baby. I knew so little about him. Coburg wasn't even his real name. Obituary says that he was Michael Cobourg-Strauss, a member of one of the wealthiest families of Austria and Bohemia. Michael's uncle, Karl Cobourg-Strauss, has been a friend of Erik's for 30 years. E has proposed to assume the child as his. Our marriage and our intimacy, though, will never be the same."

# Chapter 6

Lucas knew he was in trouble. He had heard of Singapore justice towards people caught with drugs. He was scared. He could not fathom that his Indonesian hosts had planted heroin in the bag of coffee, but apparently they had. They had surely counted on him getting through customs without inspection and that the man at the airport would succeed in getting Lucas to the car. Knowing what hotel he would be at - he recalled he mentioned it at lunch the day before he left - they could divert his luggage or carry-on bag somehow and extract the bag of heroin before Lucas would discover anything. It was undoubtedly judged by somebody as being worth the gamble. If the young man was caught, they would deny being in any way involved. Who was it? The old man? Couldn't be. He had a dozen companies that deal internationally. His drivers? His bodyguards? They seemed to be everywhere when we met. Could have been any one of them.

He went through the scenario over and over in his mind. Nobody witnessed the gift of the little bag at the airport. The driver had not given his name. The car arranged by his hosts for the trip to the airport was a black Mercedes, just like hundreds of them there - everybody's favorite muscle car in Jakarta.

Lucas was put into a cell at police headquarters. Fortunately, he was alone and thankful he would not have to be with other people in a common cell. He was advised he could make one phone call that evening. He placed a call to his mother in England, managed to explain the situation, and asked her to reach his father's brother, Richard, in Munich. His uncle Richard was a respected and well-connected lawyer. He was the only lawyer in the family and represented, in Lucas' view, the most appropriate person to find a way to somehow get him out of this. The Singapore authorities proposed a local lawyer to advise him, but Lucas had little confidence in this as a solution.

Lucas' father, Georg Brandt, had been estranged from him, his sister and his mother for years. He lived in Buenos Aires as head of Siemens in Argentina with a second wife. It would be too much for him to ask his mother to contact him about this. They had not spoken in years. Elizabeth, however, had maintained a warm relationship with his uncle Richard and his wife over the years. His father would find out about the situation in due course, but this called for a lawyer he could trust.

"Mother, I am in Singapore and I am in trouble. I'm in jail."

Elizabeth Black interrupted Lucas as he sought to explain. "What? Jail? In Singapore? I thought you were in New York or

Washington. What could you possibly have done to be in jail in Singapore?"

Suspecting that the call might be monitored, he had decided to explain his view of his situation in the call. "I have been duped. Some people in Jakarta decided to use me as an unwitting courier for heroin into Singapore, believe it or not. I accepted a small gift that I thought was quite innocent – a nice gesture from some people I had met on the visit. It was supposed to be a bag of special Javanese coffee. You know how I love coffee. But it was special, to be sure, and turned out to be not only coffee, according to my captors here. They say there was a bag of heroin hidden inside it and they brought it out for me to see....."

"Oh, my God, Lucas......"

"Somehow the customs official at the airport here suspected something and had my carry-on bag searched. They were checking maybe one in twenty-five passengers. I happened to be one of the random picks, as far as I could tell. I guess the security scanners at Jakarta airport could not detect a bag in a bag and the traffickers most likely knew it. They took the chance the bag of heroin would not be detected and could retrieve it after I arrived. A man was waiting for me with a sign and surely a car at the airport. I happened to see him through the glass of the customs section while I was in line. That was not supposed to be. I had not arranged for anyone to pick me up at the airport."

"So, Mother, to say the least, I need help - legal help - and I need it quickly. Could you call Richard in Munich? He will know what to do. I don't know where else to turn. I don't have a lot of money for this, but that is the least of my worries right now. I have to leave you now. The three minutes allowed for this are up. I am told I can make another call tomorrow. Apart from all this, I am fine. The cell here is a jail cell, but at least it's Singapore, not Cambodia or Bangladesh. Just the same, I can't fathom spending significant time in this place. I am innocent of all of it, as you surely must know, Mother. Please call Richard. I will try to call you again tomorrow. I may have to ask you to call my boss in Washington. He will have to be told something, and soon. Ring you tomorrow. Love ya, mum."

Elizabeth Black, formerly Elizabeth Black Brandt before her divorce from Lucas' father in 1984 - when Lucas was twelve and his sister nine - was a school teacher in Ealing, west of London. She and Lucas had a strong mother-son relationship. It had been forged over the years after Georg's abandonment of everyone for a Venezuelan woman twenty years younger than she, who was now his wife and with whom he had three children. He had been out of Elizabeth's and her children's lives for close to fifteen years.

Elizabeth took a deep breath, wondering how all this could have happened to her son. He had been doing so well. Good job with the World Bank. Travelling the world. Living in Washington; managing to come see her and Chris frequently as he passed through London to and from assignments in various parts of the world. Gets set up by some drug traffickers. So stupid. So dreadful. Need to call Richard.

Richard Brandt was the second of Erik and Isabel Brandt's three sons. He was a partner in a Munich law firm specializing in intellectual property. The oldest son, Georg, Lucas' father and an engineer, had joined Siemens after graduating from university and had worked for the company his entire career. He had met Elizabeth when both were working at a hotel in Gstaad one summer during their university years.

The third son, Karl, was a family doctor in a small town not far from Munich, and had remained close to Richard since childhood. The relationship with their only sister, Claudia, who was much younger than all of them, had never been close. Claudia had been born during the period when the boys were in boarding school. When the boys' parents decided to live apart, she stayed with their mother, with the boys eventually spending most of their holidays with their father in Bonn or at summer camps, most often in Canada and New Hampshire. They hardly knew their sister. She had been difficult as a child and remained that way, rebelling against authority, particularly that of her father. Claudia's antagonism toward their father, most likely initiated by their reclusive and bitter mother, had reared itself in her teens. It culminated in her decision to run away and marry, against her father's wishes, a person who was generally viewed by everyone in the family as an unsavory character.

Richard had always appreciated his young half-British nephew, although they had not seen each other in some years. Smart, engaging, considerate, more British than German, but respectful of his German heritage, Lucas as a boy had a special relationship with his grandfather. On numerous summer vacations on the island they were inseparable. Erik had taken to the little boy and was devastated when Georg and Elizabeth had broken up. Elizabeth moved back to England to be near her own family, taking Lucas and the boy's sister Chris with her. Both Erik and Richard had had but infrequent contact with Lucas since the breakup, although the old man had managed to follow the comings and goings of his now 27 year old grandson.

Richard was sure the boy was innocent of any wrong-doing in Singapore. Southeast Asia could be a sink-hole of unsavory happenings. It was not Shangri-La. One had to be careful. Lucas was the unwitting accomplice of the Chinese underworld for a few hours, with no inkling of it at all. Of that he was sure. He knew that getting Lucas out of his predicament in Singapore would be difficult. They were extremely strict about drugs. They showed no mercy. Young people had been executed for drug trafficking. He placed a call to his father at the villa on the island off the coast of Italy.

"Dada, something dreadful has happened to Lucas..." and proceeded to explain to his father what he had learned in the call from Elizabeth.

Erik was taken aback. He had not seen his grandson in over five years. "Oh, my God. This can't be. Lucas cannot possibly be involved in something like this - drug-running out of Indonesia? Impossible."

"I'm afraid I will have to take this on, even if it is not in my area of the law," Richard explained to his father. "Much too serious to leave this to someone else. Any ideas on your end, given your experience with that area of the world in the past? We may need some help. In the meantime, I am booking a flight to Singapore as soon as I can."

Erik ran through some thoughts in his mind. "I may have an idea on how to deal with this, Richard. Let me think about it. I will call you later. Let me know when you plan to leave."

Right after the call, Richard called his travel agent and booked a flight to Singapore for the following day. His partners would have to fill in for him until further notice. He figured it could take awhile. But this needed to be dealt with quickly. He would see Lucas and go from there.

Erik Brandt, at 82, had been out of government service for over seventeen years. His wife, Isabel, from whom he had been estranged since the late '70's, had died of a stroke the year before. In the years after his separation from her, Erik had eventually taken up with a companion who had passed away suddenly in 1997 of leukemia, which had overtaken her quickly. He lived alone. Within a year of Isabel's death, he had worked out a plan to dispose of most of the properties he owned and invest the proceeds in a trust fund for his children. The island property in the Tyrrhenian Sea with the castle-like villa was the only property he was keeping and it was where he lived. His daughter Claudia, who was not his real daughter, had married a dreadful character from Marseille and had generally cut herself off from the rest of the family. The only contact she kept was with Karl, the youngest of his boys. The daughter of the nephew of Karl Cobourg-Strauss, his friend from university, had turned out to be a difficult child and was just as problematic as an adult. The boys, as far as he could tell, had never learned that he was not Claudia's real father. He was not entirely sure, however, that Claudia had remained unaware of who her real father was. Isabel would have had ample opportunity over the years to open up to her. It was not something Erik could feel totally comfortable about.

Lucas' affair worried him. He needed help and Erik thought he could provide it. As he dwelled on possible ways of dealing with this, it dawned on him that it could be time to cash in on a favor from an old diplomatic acquaintance. Stanley - Stanley He from his days in Brussels - now a semi-retired senior advisor to the Minister of Justice of Singapore. Thirty years before, Stanley had been the young deputy chief of mission of Singapore to the European Commission when Erik had been the senior representative of Germany to that body. Erik had befriended the young Singapore lawyer and diplomat in Brussels and had helped him with a personal financial problem. It had involved an injudicious real estate investment the young diplomat had made in Germany. Erik had found the young man a lawyer who managed to get the affair resolved without embarrassing Stanley's employer and threatening his career. They had stayed in touch over the years. He could possibly ask Stanley to see what he could do, but, first of all, Richard would have to ascertain the strength of the case against Lucas. He called Richard and told him he would meet him in Singapore.

---

Lucas had many things to decide and arrange for. His job. Over, most likely. The World Bank could not keep anyone on staff, even on unpaid leave, who was under indictment for drug trafficking, however dubious the circumstances. Hopefully, he could get some understanding from his boss and a stay of any decision on status. Probably beyond hope.

Shit! What a dummy I was! A bag of coffee! I should have suspected something was wrong. Those Chinese guys were multi-millionaires, and they were giving me a farewell gift of a bag of coffee probably worth no more than a dollar or two? What a dunce! I should have thrown it in the first trash can I saw in the airport.

# Chapter 7

Claudia Brandt was born in April, 1968. Her brothers Georg, Richard and Karl were at school in Berne, but were all overjoyed with the news they had a little sister. That they were eighteen, sixteen and thirteen years older than the little girl did nothing to dampen their joy and anticipation in seeing the little addition to the family at Easter Break.

Despite the enthusiasm for the birth of their sister, the boys never managed to develop a close relationship with the little girl as she was growing up. They were gone most of the time and summers were taken up by activities mostly away from the house their mother and sister occupied, out of the way in the depths of southern France. At the same time, their mother had grown distant from them. On visits home, she seemed to care less and less about their studies, their well-being, their happiness, and had became increasingly withdrawn into astrology, gardening, poetry and the writing of what seemed to them, strange short stories. Karl, the youngest, was the only one of the boys who their mother seemed to cuddle, hug and confide in when they were around. They in turn increasingly went their own way - Georg passionate about football and building things, eventually becoming an engineer; Richard, the studious one, who devoured every book he laid his hands on and became the closest of the boys to their father, and Karl the happy one who wanted to be a healer and eventually became a doctor, working summers as a lifeguard at the town swimming pool in St-Remy. Georg and Richard loved their summers in America in the 1960's and early 1970's, alternating between the camp on Lake Winnipesaukee in New Hampshire and at Camp Tawingo, near Canada's Algonquin Park.

### St-Remy de Provence, September 1978

"You never loved me, Erik. You have loved your job, your honor, your standing in your diplomatic world, but you have never loved me."

Isabel glared across the table at Erik, who had arrived late the previous evening from Bonn.

"You have never really cared for me, other than materially. You are never here. You don't give a damn about my happiness. And that goes for your daughter as well."

"Not true, Isabel."

She would not let him continue.

"I was the pretty, reserved woman who you married to have sons with. I gave you that but you never gave me anything back in terms of any real love. Throughout our marriage, you have really only been interested in recovering the honor and lost standing of your father. It was about overcoming your problem with your brother being a Nazi and what he was involved with, although that has always been unclear to me about it being all that bad. Thousands, millions of Germans have had to deal with their Nazi skeletons, however large or small."

Erik looked at her, began to speak, but Isabel cut him off before he had a chance to start. "The boys were everything. You didn't care about me. You haven't cared about Claudia, despite your vow to take her as your daughter." She continued, hardly pausing at all, "Yes, I did betray you. I had an affair. You drove me to it, Erik. You have no idea how lonely I was at that time, and how disappointed I have been in our life ever since. I regret having stayed with you. I saw that ambition of yours, that damned ambition, but I believed you would get over it and come to me. You never did. You stay in Bonn, you travel the world, you devote yourself to that damned government of yours. You sent the boys away to school against my wishes - they were to receive the proper German schooling - a French lycée was not good enough for you. They went off, they grew up far from me. I hardly know them now."

"Get out. I want you to leave. I will manage. Leave Claudia and I alone. I don't care what you do with your money, with whatever else you have. Just leave me alone in this house."

"I am sorry, Isabel. I cannot undo what I have done. I suspect you would not accept now what I have not provided you over the years. I accept that I have not treated Claudia as a true daughter. She was not mine and that has haunted me." The distinguished, usually composed Erik Brandt was bent over and close to tears.

"Just the same, despite your anger and dismay with me, I will try to make amends. I will in no way leave either of you without means or be excluded from our financial affairs. As to our relationship, even if I tried to show you love now, I fear you would not accept it. That is the way it will be, I guess." Erik paused a moment, then in a low voice whispered "As you wish, I will go."

Erik rose from the table and left.

---

Ten months later, in the summer of 1979, Erik had decided that it was time to end the charade of his failed marriage. He had not spent a night at the house in St-Remy since the last encounter with Isabel. He accepted that she would not grant him a divorce, but the relationship with Anna, who he had been seeing for two years, could not be concealed anymore. He decided it was time to make official their separation and he hoped that Isabel would accept it. He rose early and drove to St-Remy the next day.

"Isabel, it is time we recognize our estrangement and move on. It is time we come to a resolution. You don't want to have anything to do with me. You made that clear to me the last time we got into this. We have certainly not been husband and wife in any way for years. We are in two different worlds. I have not wanted to provoke anything in this regard to date out of consideration for Claudia, as long as she was a child and could count on a father and brothers. She is no longer a child now. She is an adolescent and a precocious one at that. She has little affinity or even contact with the boys. That being said, this is about us, not the children. They are all old enough to deal with what our relationship has become."

"What do you propose, Erik? You obviously have something in mind. I won't give you a divorce. That is out of the question. What is it? I suppose this is being driven by your paramour?"

"No, Isabel, it is not. She is not part of this. There is no move on her part to profit in any way from the relationship. She has been married before, as you probably know by now through the boys, and has her own inheritance from her deceased husband. She doesn't need anything from me, except friendship."

"And sex, of course," shot Isabel.

"My dear, you and I have not been intimate for years. I will not bore you with the details or deny an intimate relationship with Anna. We are friends and casual lovers, if you will. We don't live together and are discreet. She has her own place. She does not come to functions with me. We stay out of the public eye. I have never sought to embarrass you, Isabel. But it is time to move on. I want to protect you financially through what I propose, by the way. You will not suffer financially."

"Well, what is it you propose?"

"A legal separation. Here in France, legal separation ends the duty of cohabitation, but the duties of assistance continue. At the financial level, the duty to support the spouse is maintained. Legally, your rights to the assets of the matrimonial union are not changed."

"Erik, I don't really care anymore. You do what you want. You can't hurt me financially, in any case. We are married. We never drew up a marriage contract. Our marriage is governed by a *régime matrimonial communal* - a communal regime. So, just as well."

"I'm sorry, Isabel. We loved each other. At least I did. We grew apart. You have always said it was my fault. You are probably right."

"Yes, Erik, there was magic between us at the start. There was passion, there was joy, laughter. But somewhere in that time you became obsessed with your family legacy - the honor of your father's name - your real name - Erik Bendt. You had changed it, but you were still a Bendt. Your brother's actions haunted you. You were petrified that people would find out who you were - who your brother was. You were going to make sure you had an impeccable career, an impeccable name, worthy of your father. It was an obsession with you and it probably still is; nothing tells me it is anything different with you today. I wanted us to enjoy life, to attend the theatre, to do things with my artist friends from Interlaken, those friends we had in Bonn when you joined the diplomatic service."

Isabel paused for a moment, but did not want to stop.

"When you were that young teacher back in Switzerland, we did so many fun things together. We would get into bed at the drop of a hat. Every year we would go to Montreux for a weekend and to Chamonix for ski weekends. We would go to Annecy, have dinner on a terrace along the canal, take a *pension* and make love all weekend long. We would go up to Gstaad on summer days, stop by a meadow on the side of the hill, take our bottle of *vin ordinaire* and a baguette for a wonderful little picnic lying in the flowers looking up at the sky with the incredible scenery all around us. We had that and then we didn't. The boys were born, you were engrossed in your reputation build - I don't know what else to call it - and I was left behind. You even took the boys away from me. You deserved to be cuckolded, Erik. I have never been sorry about my fling in Vienna, about the wonderful week I spent with that young man. He had a passion for me. He cared. He devoured me through his caring, his tenderness, his listening. I spoke, I expressed myself - he listened. You did not. Your career was more important. Your legacy. Well, that is the story of our life for the last 15 years. If you want to have this separation, fine. We are separated in any case."

Isabel went on. "As to Claudia, she is ungovernable, as you know of course and lament. At times out of control. She hates our situation - living in the middle of nowhere in the south of France. Supposed to be Shangri-La, but it's not for her. Living with an unhappy, melancholic poet and gardener, which I have become, my dear Erik. Can you blame her? An unhappy mother and an indifferent father. She is an angry young lady. She doesn't know that her father is really not her father and I have no intention of telling her. I just hope you find a way to get back into her life. She did nothing to deserve being born into this unhappy union or whatever you want to call it."

"Go. Go back to Bonn and to your girl-friend. Send me whatever papers there are for this separation. If it softens your guilt, proceed. I don't see what other purpose it has, but do it. I won't object. Now leave me alone."

It had become obvious to the Brandt boys that their father was seeing another woman. He was discreet about it and had refrained from causing any embarrassment to their mother, to them and to the lady in question, who later they got to know and appreciate. One day when they were all together for a father-sons reunion in Bonn later that summer of 1979, their father announced that he and their mother were separating. A divorce was out of the question as their mother, a devout Catholic, would not bring herself to grant Erik that request. He told the boys, 28, 26, and 23 by this time, that the relationship he had with another woman was a happy one, and that he was preparing to retire.

# Chapter 8

## Savona, Italy, July 1984

The bar in the port area was closing. It was close to 3 AM on a hot summer night. There were only four people along with the bartender left in the place. All other employees had left. A man sitting alone at a table, clearly drunk, was berating another standing a few feet away who had been moving to leave. "You, dago! Ugly piece of shit. Why you look at me?"

The short dark-haired man approached the wiry, balding drunk with the Eastern European accent. "What did you call me, you little slug?" he replied as he moved toward the table.

"Fucking dago. Scum of the earth. To hell with you."

André Gralla turned, looking to see who was watching. The bartender's back was turned and had apparently not noticed the exchange. André motioned to his cousins Marco and Luca Scalia, rising from a table around the corner of the L-shaped bar to pay their bill, that he would be going outside. He suggested with a nod that they could follow and give him a hand if needed in his altercation with the drunken interloper.

"Outside, little man. Let's go outside," challenged André. He grabbed the man by the arm and dragged him to the door. The short wiry Eastern European shook free but followed André to the door, scowling as they reached the deserted street. Three feet outside the door, André grabbed the shorter man by the collar and shoved him up against the wall. The knife had seemingly come from nowhere, with the upward thrust barely missing André's face. He backed away, crouching, as he prepared to avoid the next sweeping thrust of the knife that he knew would come. As he caught the man's forearm to block the slash of the long switchblade, the surly, staggering man was caught from behind in a bear hug by Marco who had followed them out the door. With André's twist of the man's arm, the knife dropped to the pavement. As Marco held the man, immobilizing him, André directed a hard punch to the man's face. The man turned his head at the last instant and the blow crashed instead into the side of his head. The short, slight man twitched an instant in Marco's arms, went limp, then fell to the ground.

Marco took the man's pulse, draw back an eyelid and saw that the man was dead. "He's dead, André. *Porca puttana.* Holy shit. Man, you just killed this guy."

"Oh, my God," whispered André as he crouched over the prone body of the man with blood slowly dripping from his ear. "What are we going to do?"

By this time, his cousin Luca had reached the scene after staying behind to pay the bill. "Guys, god-damn it. What the fuck have you done?" as he observed the man lying on the street. "We can't be associated with something like this..... He bent over to look more closely. "The guy's dead, for God's sake." Both Luca and his brother were known to the *carabinieri* in their home city of Genoa and had been on the edge of the law ever since their teens. Some people in Genoa considered the Scalia brothers to be part of the local mafia. In essence they were, doing loan-sharking, petty extortion and drug-dealing on a small-scale, while working as carpenters in their day jobs. This was not Genoa, though, and as far as they knew, they were unknown in the town. For one, it was the first time they had ever been in the bar they had just left. The cousins had agreed to get together in the port town, allowing André to avoid driving all the way from Marseille to Genoa, and found the bar after having dinner earlier that evening in a *ristorante* on the main square of the town.

"He's Romanian. Or was, anyway. Probably with a ship docked here," observed Marco as he looked through the items in the man's wallet.

André looked around, up and down the street, up towards windows above the street. No lights were on. "Did you see if there was anybody in that place with him?"

"I didn't notice anyone, but then again, I didn't really notice the guy or how long he had been there," replied Marco.

"Well, we need to move quickly. Anybody could come along. Somebody walking their dog or whatever," interjected Luca. "André, where is your car? We will put him in the trunk.

We have to get him out of this place. If we leave him here, the *caribinieri* will most certainly check with the bar in the morning. The bartender will remember us, although I'm not sure he saw any of the exchange inside. He didn't seem to pay any attention. He was closing up and the music was still on...... You will follow us. There is a place outside of Genoa where we can dispose of the body."

"My car? Why my car? You guys know Genoa and the area. Your car is right around the corner," replied André.

"You killed him, André. It is going to be your car. Understand? Go get the car now and you will follow us. Now! We can't afford to wait here with this body on the street. Move." Luca, the elder of the two Scalia brothers, was indignant. He knew the only way for them to avoid being accused of murder or being accessories to it was to dispose of the body where it would never be found. The Romanian needed to disappear.

**Saint-Cyr-sur-Mer, France, five years later.....**

As a boy, André Gralla had always dreamed of marrying a blond, blue-eyed beauty who was, in his dreams, always taller than he. As he contemplated the features of the young lady across the table from him, thoughts of his boyhood fantasy crossed his mind. Here was the image of that dream, right in front of him. The girl was blond with great big dreamy blue eyes, and had an incredible figure. She was beautiful. And she was taller than he. He had met her the night before at the party at his friend J.J.'s place outside of Toulon. She had worn a frilly short skirt that barely reached mid-thigh and a halter that did not cover all that much. Beautiful. A real dish, as an American friend once said about a girl on the beach at Tropez.

She was quite drunk by the time they reached his apartment. They had been among the last to leave his friend's apartment. André's own pad on the top-floor of an apartment building up a steep hill overlooking the bay was midway between Toulon and Marseille. Within minutes of arriving around 3 AM, the girl had passed out on the futon next to the bay window. André put a blanket over her, poured himself an orange juice, and went to bed.

The stunning young girl with the big blue eyes was now wearing one of his shirts, sipping a *café au lait* and wondering where she was.

---

André was of Jewish and Italian ancestry. His father had managed to hide his Jewish heritage all his adult life. André had done nothing to correct this, to set the record straight. It was better to leave it alone. He had no desire to re-establish his Jewish roots. His mother was from Genoa and part of a large Italian Catholic family and as far as he knew, never learned her husband was Jewish. She died when André was seven years old. He had hardly known her. His father, who had not remarried – he was 40 when his wife died - had been in the clothing business in Marseille and had died ten years before, leaving André the business, which had been struggling for years. The big

50

department stores of Europe and America were increasingly buying direct now from China, India, Bangladesh, Thailand and so on. Intermediaries like André and his father before him were being squeezed out of the business. To spread risk, André had invested in real estate and in a share in a restaurant in Marseille, both of which were not doing much better than his clothing business. He kept lawyers busy in warding off creditors and the people he had managed to cheat over the years. He also had something in his past he was always concerned about. His cousins, Marco and Luca had disposed of the body. There were no witnesses. The crewman from the Romanian freighter had disappeared. At the time, Marco tracked the newspaper of Savona: the disappearance had been reported with speculation that the missing crewman had fallen into the bay and the body washed out to sea with the tide. André had heard nothing about it since then. Nevertheless, his cousins had intimated that he would have to be careful. They were witnesses to his killing a man and had let it be known that they would use it, relative or no relative, if he ever crossed them. André knew a lot about the shady activities of his cousins and they knew he knew. The uneasy relationship between he and the Scalia boys had existed for years.

André had learned as a boy that his father's father, his paternal grandfather, had been a prosperous manufacturer of kitchen utensils - pots and pans and knives and forks - in Czechoslovakia before the war. He was a descendant of a family of traders in silver and other precious metals that had operated in

Bohemia for centuries, but had perished with André's grandmother and the rest of their extended family without a trace in 1941. His father had escaped the holocaust through a fortunate association with a businessman in the clothing trade. At eighteen, he had taken a job with a clothing merchant and friend of his father in Prague who had dealings throughout Europe. In 1936 and well before the war, he had been sent to Marseille to help oversee the man's dealings in France. Marseille was an important hub in the clothing trade that flowed through one end of the Mediterranean to the other.

His father, Joseph, had hidden his Jewish ancestry ever since arriving in France. He had last seen his parents and sisters on a trip home in 1937. Joseph had related to André how he had repeatedly implored his father to sell his manufacturing operations and get out of the center of Europe. The operations included plants in Plzen and Bratislava and Krackow in Poland. Hitler was railing against Jews and making claims on lands where Germans formed large parts of the population. Czechoslovakia was one of them, with over 25% of the population being ethnic German. His father had estimated the value of Maurice Gralla's manufacturing empire at well over 500 million francs in 1937. But the old man had been stubborn; the business was his life and he refused to give much credence to the threats to the Jewish community. The Jewish community of Prague was a part of the city's history. Relations with the rest of the population were cordial and harmonious. There were no real problems for the

Jews in Czechoslovakia. There had not been any pogroms or repressions of the Jews in Bohemia since well before the turn of the century. Old Maurice did not, would not, see it coming.

Only after the war did his father learn that the Gralla company had been confiscated by the Nazis in 1941, with the plants re-tooled to produce shell casings for the German army. Every one of the Gralla company plants had been converted to war production and were ultimately destroyed by the allies in the bombing runs of Czech munitions plants in 1944 and 1945. As to the extended Gralla family as well as the Gersten family of his grandmother, they all disappeared without a trace. The family fortune disappeared with the loss of all of these relatives. André's father had been bitter about this all his life. He blamed himself for not being more insistent with his father on getting out when it was possible. As André had gotten older, he had wondered what his own life would be like if the family heritage had not been destroyed by a German madman and his henchmen 50 years before.

---

The girl here in his apartment looked to be German or Swedish or Dutch, but her French was, well ....French.

*"Ou est-ce que je suis?* Where am I? How did I get here?"

"We are at my apartment in Saint-Cyr-sur-Mer and we came here after the party at around 3. It is now 10 o'clock. We got here in my car. *Ça va?* Are you OK?"

"I have somewhat of a headache, but I will be OK." She paused, then looked at André. "I don't remember getting here. You didn't take me to your bed, by the way. That's surprising. Why? Most guys I meet do their best to get me into their bed. But you didn't."

"You were out of it. Would not have been much fun....I can understand what you say about the guys, though. I won't comment any further."

"What do you mean by that?" Claudia looked up, looking offended.

"Well, what you are wearing under my shirt. But anyway, if you are offended, I apologize." André paused a moment, then continued, "Some more coffee?"

Claudia ignored the question, fidgeted a bit, looked around the apartment, pushed back her chair, and then declared "I must be going. Have to find my car. Must be still back where the party was. I guess I didn't tell you that I had a car."

"You didn't tell me much at all at the party, and nothing afterwards – you were 'out'. We exchanged names – yours is Claudia. Do you remember mine, by the way? If you don't, it is André and good morning, stunning blond girl with the big blue eyes. Please sit down. We don't have to leave just yet. To refresh your memory, we were having a good time at J.J.'s; at least I was and I thought you were too. We had some good laughs when the music was eventually turned down low and laughed at some crazy stories from the guy with the handlebar mustache. After

54

awhile, though, you were fast asleep at the end of the couch. Everyone had to leave around two – J.J. was throwing us out – he wanted to crash, so I brought you here. So, where do you have to be?

"I don't really have to be anywhere but I must go, just the same."

Claudia rose up from the table and pressed her hair back. "I have an apartment in Montpellier. But, if you really want to know....I spend a lot of time at my mother's house in the country near St-Remy de Provence. I was going to go there later."

"So, you live with your mother? No boyfriend?"

"No. No boyfriend. Not these days, anyway. And yes, I guess you could say I live with my mother.  She is getting on. She is in her 60s but going on 80 and a bit out of it, in her own little world of gardening, Indian music and poetry. She has been diagnosed with an early onset of Alzheimer's. She forgets things. I spend a lot of time these days taking care of her. The place is cozy, a bit secluded. I have the run of it. I used to paint a lot – it's a great place for that."

André continued his questioning. "Do you work? Are you a student? What do you do?"

"I don't have a job right now. I had one for awhile, doing graphics for an advertising firm in Montpellier, but they let me go a couple months ago, just before I was to become full-time. You probably know how that goes with young people starting out here in France. Work on a six month internship, go on unemployment, get another internship for six months, then go back on unemployment. Employers can't afford to keep us on longer. Stay longer than six months, they can't fire you. Almost a miracle if you become full-time."

"Yes, I know all about that. I have a business. I import men's clothing from Asia. I only hire people with at least ten years experience in the trade, and only when things are going well, which they are not right now. I certainly can't afford to hire someone out of university or trade school. Train them for three months, then have to let them go before six months is up. If they are with me longer than that, I'm stuck with them. Crazy laws we have here in France."

Claudia continued. "So, the job was bound to end anyway and the director of advertising wanted to take me to bed. I put him off. It couldn't last, and it didn't."

"I can take you to your car. We can have some lunch on the way there, though. You can leave for St-Remy after that. Are you on? I'm buying."

*"Oui, Monsieur André,* I accept."

It was the first smile she had shown since about 1 AM the evening before. The lady was relaxing a bit. Maybe this really could go further, thought André. She is a sight to behold. Need to pursue this.

"You can keep my shirt on for the restaurant, by the way. The halter may be a little provocative for my good friend Gino, the womanizing owner of the restaurant where we will be having lunch. He's absolutely lecherous despite being a great chef and a good friend. Better you cover up or he will not leave us, meaning you, alone."

"Whatever you say."

André and Claudia arrived at Gino's and sure enough, Gino visually undressed Claudia and joined them at their table. After a few minutes of friendly banter and finally a look from André to back off from getting too close to the girl, Gino rose and went off to greet other customers.

"*Alors, monsieur André*, do you know anybody who could need somebody like me? I really do need a job. My father has been angry with me for quitting university. He said he didn't like the crowd I was hanging out with, so he cut my allowance in half. The job with the advertising firm was OK while it lasted, but that is over. The apartment, food, car and other expenses I have add up to a lot more than the allowance I have. And I don't want to go back and live with my mother. I could find a sugar-daddy for my keep somewhere. Do you know a *vieux monsieur riche* who could be my sugar daddy?" she said with a mocked little girl blinking of the eyes over pursed lips.

André thought about it. She could maybe work for me. I will see how the relationship develops. What a babe she is, though. Don't really need anybody and can hardly afford a new addition to the payroll. But I would love to have her in my bed.

Three days later after a night of partying and love-making, André offered Claudia a job in his office in Marseille. She accepted.

At the end of her lease in Montpellier three months later, she moved in with him.

Within a month, Erik stopped sending Claudia her monthly allowance. When Erik learned of her taking the job with *Importations/Exportations Gralla*, he made some enquiries regarding the company and its owner. He learned that the company was known to have weathered financial difficulties and was often delinquent on its accounts. He also learned that André Gralla, 34 years old, had an unsavory reputation in the clothing business, was a 'man about town', a *'boulevardier'* as the French say, in the party-going crowd around the Cote d'Azur.

The company was André's third in the business, following the failures of two other companies in the past. He had apparently inherited his father's clothing import business when in his early 20's, but had run it into the ground within a couple of years.

Erik was disconsolate about what Claudia was doing and who she was working for, but tolerated the situation and continued to send Claudia her half-allowance. But when he learned she had moved in with him, that was it. He stopped payments altogether. A meeting two weeks later in Marseille turned into a shouting match.

"Daddy, you never cared for me. You never cared for Mama. You have been a real shit with us. All you ever cared about was the boys and your 'standing' and all that bullshit about being an ambassador and all of that. I don't care about your honor. And I don't need the allowance any more, by the way."

"Claudia, this man is no good for you. His businesses have failed, one after the other. You will regret this. Come to your senses, go back to university. Get your *Diplôme*. I will cover it."

"How do you know anything about André's businesses and what you say are failures? He told me he had some tough luck with previous ventures, but nothing about bankruptcies or anything about what you are inferring."

"I had somebody do some digging on him. What I found is not good. Claudia, please don't do this."

"How can you ask me to listen to you, Daddy? You have neglected Mama and I for years and now you want me to listen to you? And, you tell me you investigated my boyfriend as some criminal or fraud artist? Really, Daddy, you've gone too far." By this time, Claudia was shouting and people in the café were looking their way.

"Claudia, you will regret taking up with him," replied Erik in a tempered voice, cognizant of the disturbance the argument with his daughter was generating.

"Daddy, the discussion is over," whispered Claudia, leaning over the table with eyes blazing at her father. "I am not going to change what I am doing. I am going to help André turn things around in his business and make something of it. I hated university anyway and I can't bear the thought of going back to St-Remy. I'm sorry, Daddy. I have to go."

"What are you going to do about your mother?"

"What? You ask what I am going to do about mother?" as she rose to leave. "How can you ask me that? I will continue to see her. But she is for you to look after. Maybe it is time for you to do so now. You have been retired for years and I would think you had the time to do so."

"What I meant was the explanation of what you are doing. Not sure she will like this."

"What do you really care, Daddy, about what she thinks about what I am doing? I'm leaving."

Erik watched Claudia stride angrily down the street. She has never been my daughter, and I guess she never will be. She has always been somebody else's.

# Chapter 9

## Singapore, April 1999

"We don't care who he is or who his parents are or any of that. He was caught with heroin for the purpose of trafficking in our country. He will have to face the penalty for that. Are you his counsel? If you are not, I cannot say any more. I will only speak with Mr. Brandt's counsel. If you are that, you must be licensed to practice in Singapore. I will only speak with counsel who is licensed here. Now, are you licensed to practice law here, Herr Brandt?"

Richard Brandt understood this, of course, and replied in a forceful, lawyer-like mildly indignant posture, "No, I am not, but I will be returning with licensed counsel very soon and would like to see the proof you have on this supposed transgression."

One of Richard's associates had had dealings with a German company who had a case in Singapore and within a few hours, they reached one of the Singapore lawyers who had worked with their Hamburg associate. Richard arranged to meet an Anthony Wong the next morning. It did not take long for

Richard to ascertain the competence of the man, and they arranged to meet the assistant prosecutor the next day.

At the meeting, Anthony Wong quickly got to the point. "We need to see the proof you have and understand the circumstances of Mister Brandt's arrest. My client claims he knew nothing of the existence of the forbidden substance in the bag of coffee he received as a gift before arriving at the Jakarta airport to take a flight here."

"Counselor, the proof is uncontestable. A customs official found the bag containing the substance, pulled it from your client's carry-on luggage right before his eyes. He immediately called the customs police, they opened the bag and found the plastic bag containing a considerable amount of heroin. Proof is there. We have four witnesses to the inspection and the discovery."

Wong quickly countered. "Where did the police open the bag of coffee? In front of Herr Brandt? In the office? Where?"

"I am told - and the report says - they opened the bag of coffee and discovered the heroin in front of the accused."

Wong then said, "It is our right to see the report of proof from the police. When can we have that? I will expect it before the end of day tomorrow."

The prosecutor responded that he would have a copy of the report for pickup by Mr. Wong's paralegal at 10 AM the following day.

Erik Brandt arrived in Singapore later that afternoon. Richard met his father at the airport and in the car on the way to the hotel discussed what he had learned. The information was sketchy as he and the local lawyer had not yet seen the police report. There was not much they could do in the meantime. At dinner that evening, they decided that Erik's presence in Singapore would not be advertised in any way. Erik had placed a call to Stanley He before leaving home, saying he would be in Singapore within the next few days and that he would call him upon arriving. No mention had been made of the purpose of his visit. The retired diplomat would call his old friend once he and Richard fully understood what they were up against.

The following morning, Anthony Wong called Richard at the hotel. They agreed to meet at Wong's office at 11AM to review the report and discuss further actions.

Later, at the hotel, Richard outlined to Erik the contents of the police report. "The proof appears to be airtight, except for one thing. The report says the bag of coffee was opened in front of Lucas and the plastic bag of heroin extracted right then. Wong says that Lucas told him no one opened the coffee bag in front of him. He says the customs policeman came out of the back office with a plastic bag containing a white substance in one hand and the larger opened brown paper coffee bag in the other, and summoned what appeared to be a superior. At that point, Lucas was brought back into the office where he was charged."

Erik saw an opening. "This may be the fault line in their case, Richard. If we can somehow ascertain that the police did indeed open the coffee bag and find the heroin in the back office and not in front of Lucas as they contend in their report, we may have a case." With this observation, Erik believed there could be a way out.

"Father, we think alike. It may be the only thing we have in Lucas' defense. Lucas admitted to putting the brown bag in his carry-on after receiving it at the airport in Jakarta, so we cannot claim it was put there without his knowledge. The heroin was probably in the bag at that time, given that a man was waiting for Lucas at his arrival, something Lucas had not expected. It does add up to a plant with an unsuspecting young Westerner. But, the police may have blundered here if the heroin was actually in the coffee bag and they extracted it without Lucas being present. The proof could be contested. We need to discredit the testimony of the customs police."

"Private investigator, Richard," quickly replied Erik. "We need to have your local colleague hire one and hopefully have him find out through his police contacts what really happened. We will have difficulty in getting the police to admit error in this without some sort of proof that the process was tainted."

Richard, smiling back at his father: "Un-huh. Good idea, Father. I think you are right. You would have made a good lawyer yourself, as I have always told you."

"Thank you, son," replied Erik, with a smile, continuing with his view on what to do. "If we can get a credible report that what Lucas says about the process of him being shown the bag of heroin, at least an indication of corroboration of it from the inside of the customs police force, I can go to my old friend. With perhaps enough material to have the accusation thrown out on technical grounds. But without a credible report from an investigator along the lines we are talking about, Stanley would be in a tough position to do anything."

"Agreed. Let's proceed. I will see Anthony again this afternoon."

---

"Anthony, I am not really concerned with the cost. I need the best private investigator you know. It has to be done judiciously and quickly," said Richard as he met with the Singapore lawyer later that day.

"Sir, I know exactly the right people for this. Trust me."

Ten days later, Anthony Wong was invited to the offices of East Asia Security Partners and was shown a draft of the senior investigator's report. The investigator explained that the firm had helped the customs police on a number of occasions in the past and had some IOU's they could call in. Within a few days, the lead investigator was told that the customs police were concerned that the police officer on duty at the time had not extracted the bag of heroin in front of the accused. In essence, the case could be viewed as tainted, but under pressure to score some 'finds' as they call them, they decided to accept the duty officer's report without correction. They needed an arrest. They were not meeting their numbers. Apparently, too much stuff was coming into the country. So, because the heroin was truly found in the bag of coffee, even if it was correctly extracted in front of the accused, they decided to proceed with the arrest.

Anthony Wong requested this to be put into a signed final report and provided to him by end of day.

---

Erik Brandt called Stanley He at his office the next day and arranged for them to meet for a few minutes later that afternoon. When they met, Erik quickly got to the point. "Stanley, when I called you the other day from my home saying I was coming here to Singapore and wanted to see you, I could not tell you what my visit was truly about. I can tell you now. It is a case involving my grandson and I will be asking you to determine if and how you could help this young man, who is innocent of any wrong-doing."

"Herr Brandt, you helped me out once and I have always been thankful for it. What is this about?"

A week later, Lucas was brought to the front desk of the Singapore City Jail where the clerk announced that the charges against him were being dropped. He was free to leave.

Anthony Wong had been appraised of this in the minutes leading up to Lucas' liberation. He was informed that the Ministry of Justice had become aware of the case, the chief prosecutor for drug offences had been summoned and asked to investigate the contentions of the customs police in their report of the incident. The customs official on duty that evening ended up admitting that the bag of coffee had not been opened in front of the accused. The man insisted that the bag of heroin had come from the coffee bag, but the error in procedure he admitted to provided sufficient justification to invalidate the charges.

In a telephone call that evening, Erik told his old acquaintance "Stanley, I thank you, my friend. Without your asking questions within the system, I am sure nothing would have happened. In the end, Singapore avoided an unjust conviction. I think you know that. I am truly grateful."

"Herr Brandt, I managed to find out it was the belief of some of the officials involved in the case that your grandson was probably telling the truth about the incident, but there was this bag of heroin just the same. All they needed was the technicality to overturn the decision. I gave them the track to follow based on what you told me. There is great pressure on the customs police to get arrests in this cancerous drug trade that is everywhere in this area of the world. In the end, an innocent young man has been spared to live his life. I am glad to have contributed to this. What you did for me 30 years ago saved my reputation and most probably my career. I am most happy to have repaid the eternal debt that I had towards you."

"Stanley, my friend, we must continue to stay in touch. I am getting on in years, but intend to remain active and involved in this world. You will always be welcome at my home. The place has some charm, and I invite you to come the next time you are in Europe. You know how to reach me."

"I graciously accept. We will speak soon. Have a safe trip back, and make sure your grandson stays out of trouble and away from shady Asians, I am afraid."

"*Auf Wiedersehen*, Stanley. Until we meet again."

---

After Lucas was freed, Erik had him stay with him at his hotel over the 36 hours between his release and their respective flights out of the country. Richard took the first flight available for Munich. He had been away for over three weeks and had to get back to his practice.

Grandfather and grandson spent most of the next day and a half conversing about life, career, and family. It had been close to ten years since they had spent any time together, certainly five since they had seen each other. Lucas had never been told of his grandfather's youth, his time in Germany, as a teacher in Switzerland, and his return to Germany to work in the diplomatic service. His own father had never explained much of this to him, and his mother had never known much of it.

During the time over meals and long talks on the terrace of the hotel in the afternoon and late evenings, Erik told his grandson that his original name was Braun (he was not going to tell him it was really Bendt), and that his father, Richard von Braun, had been a diplomat in the service of the Kaiser leading up to and during the First World War. Lucas had always wondered where the numerous properties of the family throughout Europe had come from. A house outside of Bonn, a property near Nuremberg, an elegant house in Munich not far from where Richard and his wife lived. There was a villa and large property in the south of France, and an enchanting castle-like villa on an island in the Tyrrhenian Sea off the coast of Italy where he spent time as a child. Erik explained to him that his father, Richard von Braun, had come into possession of all of it before the Great War through the inheritance of his wife who had come from a very wealthy family from Munich. Lucas learned that his grandfather's brother had done some things to cast shame on the Braun name - his grandfather wouldn't say what those were - and for this reason, Erik had left Germany for Switzerland and had his name changed to Brandt. He had met Lucas' grandmother, Isabel, who had passed away the year before, one summer in Gstaad after the war when she was a student from a small town in Bavaria. She was working at a hotel for the summer, and he was on holiday from his job teaching at the Gymnasium in Interlaken. They had married in France in 1949. When asked by Lucas why he returned to Germany to work in the diplomatic service in 1952, leaving the prosperity and tranquility of Switzerland, Erik responded by saying it was a question of honor. His father had been a diplomat. He had been a true German patriot, had deplored the Nazis and their reign, and had died in shame of what had happened to the Fatherland. Erik felt compelled to honor his legacy, even if he had changed his name.

He explained that there were not many people who were alive in 1952 who had not been part of the Nazi regime, were not viewed or suspected of being communist sympathizers, and could be considered to be competent enough to work in the diplomatic service of the country. Herr Adenauer, the new chancellor, was desperate to build a government of people not associated with the wartime regime and who were not communists."

"I saw the opportunity to return to the country of my birth and to continue the legacy of my father. I took it. My name change was overlooked. I was Erik Brandt and welcome to join the diplomatic service of the Federal Republic of Germany."

Lucas brought up the subject of his own father, who had been out of his life for years. "Grandfather, my father is estranged from everyone it seems. He doesn't seem to care about anyone in the family, including me, his own son. Aunt Claudia is in another world. Richard and Karl seem to be close, but my father is basically absent from the family. He did pay for my university education in England, but has otherwise contributed little to my life. What happened?"

"Lucas, a lot of all this comes from me. I have just told you of my need to do what my own father did, to live up to his legacy, however misplaced that may have turned out to be in the end, as I admit now. I felt I had to do it. It was so compelling for me. And the family suffered because of it. I was gone most of the time. Your grandmother did not marry someone only to see him go off around the world for weeks at a time. She thought she was marrying a teacher in a top-tier private high school who she believed had inherited a lot of money, promising a well-off tranquil life of marital bliss and, as a devout Catholic, with many babies coming along the way. Two years into our marriage, I decided to disrupt all that, move the family to Bonn and devote my life to something other than her and our new son, your father. She put up with it for a few years; we loved each other still, but......."

"A few years after the birth of your uncle Karl, when he was ten or eleven I believe, Isabel had become completely, but completely disenchanted with living in Bonn, which is a very boring city by the way. Bureaucrats live there. Hardly anyone else does. The opportunity to occupy the villa in St-Remy had arisen in the meantime. I had rented the villa in St-Remy for years to an American couple who decided to move back to Virginia or whatever. Isabel had become an accomplished artist in the meantime, and I thought it would be good for her to get out of Bonn and so I proposed we move the family to St-Remy de Provence. She accepted and at the same time I thought it would be good to put the boys in boarding school in Berne. I could not see them going to French schools in rural Provence. So that is what we did. This would be 1965, close to thirty-five years ago."

"What this did was separate your grandmother from your father and your uncles Richard and Karl. I had not intended it to be that way, but that is what it did. I also had intended on spending more time in Provence than I did. The nature of the job evolved into one of considerable travel and time away, even more so than when we were all in Bonn. Your grandmother and I drifted apart, much as the boys drifted away from their mother. Then Claudia was born, almost thirteen years after Karl. Isabel was forty-three and I was fifty. Not a great age, at least for me, to spend time raising a little girl. Your father and your uncles at first doted on the little girl when they were at home, but they were not home all that much. Christmas, Easter, a long weekend here and there, with most of their summers at camp in America and Canada. St-Remy de Province was not an exciting place for them to be, I must say."

"You ask about your father in all of this. Your father was always ambitious and even as a young boy, was bossy. He bullied his brothers constantly. I had trouble with him. I must admit the decision to send the boys to boarding school had a lot to do with Georg's behavior. Your grandmother had difficulty in managing him in my absence. The school in Berne turned out to good for him. The people there put some discipline into the boy and I was thankful for that. But Georg was defiant with me...throughout his youth. It was not a good father-son relationship. Then, he met your mother one summer and I thought he would settle down. Elizabeth is an exceptional woman and I believe she truly loved your father. He was a handsome athletic young man, and could be quite charming. He was certainly smart and he managed to sweep your wonderful mother off her feet. But he was unfaithful, as it turned out. Elizabeth could not tolerate it, and I don't blame

72

her. After your birth and that of your sister, the relationship deteriorated. The marriage lasted eight years, I believe, but in reality, it was over two years after you were born."

"I remember summers I spent with you and father and mother on the island," Lucas said to his grandfather. "I remember arguments between the two of them - I must have been six or seven - but what I remember most were the times you and I spent in the boat you had then, fishing. I would dive off the end of the boat in some cove. You had taught me how to swim when I think I was three. I loved that. We would spend whole afternoons in the bays around the island and across the channel. I remember catching this god-awful fish that was one of those bottom scavengers. How ugly it was. It was huge and I thought we would have a feast of it at supper before I saw what it looked like when I brought it out of the water. You had a good laugh. I called you Dada in those days."

"Yes, Lucas, those days were precious. You were the first of the grandchildren and, it turns out, one of only four and the only boy. There is your lovely sister Christina, who I have not seen for a long time, either, by the way. Karl has two lovely girls, but you are the only boy and my only grandson. I wish we could have spent more time together, but I understand your mother and her taking you and Chris to England. Too bad for me."

"And too bad for me, Dada."

After a pause, Lucas asked his grandfather, "What happened with Claudia? She has always seemed to me to be so rebellious, so angry. I don't remember grandmother being that way at all. She was kind, reserved, almost pious in the times I was around her."

"I don't know, Lucas. Claudia was that way from the start, since she was a little girl," Erik replied. "To make matters worse, she married a devious crook, in my view. He is up to no good. I don't trust him with anything. She made a very bad choice. They have had a stormy relationship to begin with. I am sure there are a lot of things that I don't even know about. They have separated more than once. Claudia threw him out of the house on at least one occasion. Infidelity, I imagine. But, they end up getting back together." Erik knew that Claudia's behavior was heavily influenced by her mother's own anger with her own situation, her unhappiness with him and the marriage, her stubbornness about refusing to consider a divorce. And, Claudia was the daughter of another man, with all the inherited traits that can come from the parentage. But he was not willing to share any of this perspective with Lucas. That Claudia was the daughter of another man was a family secret and he intended to keep it that way. That Claudia was also causing him trouble about the family inheritance, was something else he kept from Lucas. The boy did not need to know any of that.

"In any case, Lucas, you are free now," Erik said, changing the subject. "You have managed to escape this hell and your life is all in front of you. Use it wisely and enjoy it...I would like to see you on the island soon. We must continue these discussions. I am very interested in what you have been doing with the World Bank. It is not far from what I spent my life doing."

"What we are going to do this evening, however, is have dinner at the Raffles. You have heard of the Raffles Hotel of Singapore, I presume?"

"Certainly I have heard of it," replied Lucas. "The famous gathering place of the Brits in Malaya before the war. It still exists? I thought it was a thing of the past."

"It is not, my dear boy, and if you can stand some of the insufferable old colonials who still hang around the place, I am told it is still quite an enjoyable place to spend an evening. I reserved a table for us at 7:30. At 6:30, we will have a drink in the Long Bar, the famous Long Bar, where I have not been in close to 30 years...We're going to the Raffles, Old Boy," declared Erik with a twist of the end of his white mustache while doing his best to mock a British upper class accent.

---

While Lucas was embroiled in his incarceration in Singapore, he was terminated from his job in Washington. Lucas' boss at the Bank, Bill Gasson, did all he could to save it for Lucas, at least until a final determination of guilt, but the legal department and the head of human resources determined that the Bank had to establish full distance from the accused employee. They couldn't have one of their employees under indictment for drug trafficking and still be on the payroll. Even suspension without pay was further than they were willing to go. The World

Bank and its employees had to be entirely above reproach or suspicion of any wrongdoing. Lucas' tenure at the World Bank was over.

Elizabeth was overjoyed when Lucas called her to say he was coming home. He had been freed. The charges were dropped.

"Mother, I am coming home. I will decide what to do from there. Grandpa and Richard were great for me. They saved my life. I will tell you all about it when I see you. Say hello to Chris and assure her all is well. I have been having a wonderful time with Grandpa since my release and we will both be leaving Singapore tomorrow. Here is my flight information.....I can take the tube to Ealing. Don't worry. See you tomorrow evening. Love ya, Mum."

"Lucas, I just got back from Washington. I managed to sell your car for a decent price and take care of the apartment lease and pay the accounts I saw in your mail. You have many friends, it appears, as you had quite a few messages on your phone. I took them all down. You should definitely call who I think was your boss from the messages on your phone. A Bill Gasson left a message saying he did not know how to get hold of you and could you please call him. He said he had an idea for next steps, so the message went. Have a safe flight home and give a big hug to your grandfather for me."

---

After arriving in London, Lucas took a week to reflect on his future and what had happened to him before following up on Bill Gasson's advice. The advice was to consider working for another international economic development organization. Bill said he knew senior people in more than a few of them and that the Singapore business did not necessarily disqualify him from employment with other organizations. The charges had been dropped, after all. People working in the international sphere knew these things could happen, and to anyone. He had offered to provide a recommendation to a former colleague who was now with the United National Industrial Development Organization, UNIDO, based in Vienna.

In mid-July, Lucas called Bill Gasson's contact at UNIDO and learned that there was a job opening for a development economist. He would need to have his resume, and they could arrange a day and time for an interview. He said that he knew Bill Gasson quite well and that Bill had indeed provided a strong recommendation regarding Lucas' capabilities and worthiness in the international development field. He also said he understood from Bill that he had come through a bit of trouble in Singapore necessitating the 'separation', as he called it, from the World Bank. He would expect to discuss that in due course. An interview in Vienna was set for August 11th. Lucas agreed to e-mail his resume before the end of the day.

In the meantime, in the weeks that followed, Lucas renewed his relationships with the family on his mother's side. He spent time with his cousins Ivan and Vincent Black, both artists in London, with whom he had shared much of his childhood. A visit and discussion with his jovial uncle David who owned an oriental carpet shop in West London, led to Lucas agreeing to look after the shop for a few days while David travelled to Turkey to purchase additions to his selection of high quality Turkish and Persian carpets.

Lucas also managed to reach Elaine, the young lady he had been seeing before travelling to Indonesia, explaining his absence. He had sent her an e-mail from the hotel in Singapore the day after he was released, but had provided little information. The e-mail had been the first communication they had in close to a month. She was shocked to hear what Lucas told her during the phone call.

"Elaine, I doubt if I will be going to D.C. very soon. I regret that our thing together didn't really get very far. I'm sorry. I will most probably be working in Europe, making it difficult for us to see much of each other." After an awkward pause, Lucas continued. "We should nevertheless stay in touch. I would like that."

"I understand, Lucas. You must have been quite scared. I'm glad you are out of that," replied the soft-spoken young American woman at the other end of the line. "I do hope you get the job. Let me know what happens." The two continued to chat for a few minutes, with Elaine closing the call with an "All the best, Lucas. Let me know when you are back state-side. Cheers."

# Chapter 10

In the week leading up to her departure for Vienna, Caroline Weber spent a day in the ivy-covered Watson Library of the University of Kansas, researching 19th century Austrian and Bohemian history. While going through sources of information, she came across the names, addresses and telephone numbers of a variety of genealogical archives for both Austria and the Czech Republic. She zeroed in on information concerning the period of 1870 to 1875.

What was happening in Austria and Bohemia at that time? What had prompted Thomas Weber and his wife Barbara to emigrate to America when they did? She realized that specific information on Thomas and Barbara, their births, marriage, what Thomas did for a living, and where they lived, would have to come from on-the-ground detailed searches of government records. Determining how he got the money to buy all the land he bought in Kansas, would be something else. Not being able to read German or Czech, she quickly surmised she would have to hire someone to research all that. One thing that caught Caroline's eye that afternoon was a reference to the Vienna Krach - the Grunderkrach market crash of May 9, 1873. The crash was the trigger of the great European depression that lasted for the better part of a decade. It led to the failure of hundreds of enterprises, banks, and financial houses in Austria and countless others elsewhere on the continent. The crash came about through a combination of rampant speculative investments in privately-financed railroads and manufacturing enterprises and a fall in the demand for silver. This followed Germany's decision to abandon the silver standard in the wake of the Franco-Prussian war of 1870-1871. The crash spread to America, leading to the failure of many banks. This included the Philadelphia banking empire of one of America's richest men, Jay Cooke who, along with his brother, had largely financed the conduct of the war effort of the northern states in the American civil war.

Back in Westmoreland at the family farm, Caroline got on the phone and managed to secure an appointment with an English-speaking archives administrator at the Municipal and Provincial Archives of Vienna for the following Tuesday, August 8th.

Finally breaking his silence on the matter of his daughter's search for the truth about the family, Raymond Weber spoke about it over dinner the evening before she left. "Caroline, I suspect you are going to find out things about your ancestor, your great-great-grandfather, that will be distasteful. My father never

80

wanted to hear anything about Thomas Weber or even talk about it. He once told me that it was best that I not know anything, as I would not like what I would learn. I don't know any of the history of him, but I hope you find out. It has always been somewhere in the back of my mind. Go to it. But be careful. You are going at this by yourself. You should let us know where you are while you are over there. You will do that. OK?"

"Yes, Dad, of course, and I will be careful. It's the only time I will be able to do this. I will discover what I discover."

Caroline arrived in Vienna a few days later. Through the hotel information kiosk at the airport, she found a small hotel off MarianhilferStrasse, a mile or so from the center of the old city, on a quiet side street with many small restaurants and shops. On Monday, she took a bus to spend the day touring the vast and imposing Schonnbrun Palace and surrounding grounds. Later, she dropped into the Greek restaurant next to the hotel and had a meal of Moussaka with a side dish of Tzatziki, both of which she had never had before. Kansas was not known for its culinary diversity.

Her meeting the next day at the archives office of Vienna led her to realize any attempt at direct research on her part would be futile. Everything there from the 1860's and 1870's was in handwritten German old script. There was no way she could see getting anywhere on her own. The administrator suggested to Caroline that she hire a researcher accustomed to the records and the writing of the time. She was given a name and telephone number. An agreement was reached quickly. The work would be concluded by the following Monday. In the meantime, she would be a tourist.

Over the next three days, Caroline embraced much of what there was for a young American to embrace in Vienna. She toured the Imperial Apartments of the Hofburg Palace, the museums of classical art and natural history, found an outdoor classical music concert for an evening of music, shopped the MarianhilferStrasse and attended a play. On Friday afternoon, as she was returning to her hotel through the Old Inner City, she observed the elegant façade of the Cafe Griensteidl, walked in and found a small table near the door.

---

Lucas Brandt had just completed his interview at the UNIDO office across the Danube. He was quite pleased with the exchange. The discussion progressed rapidly into many aspects of Lucas' work with the World Bank. They knew about the Singapore affair and that all charges were dropped, and appeared to have a glowing recommendation from Bill Gasson. The HR person ended the meeting by saying that they would be getting back to Lucas in London within two or three weeks.

Near the end of the walk back to his hotel in the old city, Lucas noticed a cafe with the name Griensteidl splashed in big letters over the door and decided to have an afternoon tea and perhaps an apple strudel. It is Vienna, after all, he thought. He found a small table not far from the door and next to one with a young woman who was engrossed in a map spread out in front of her.

Their eyes. Pretty girl, thought Lucas. They each nodded a polite hello. Lucas proceeded to order his tea and strudel and opened up the Tribune. He got through a couple of articles, then put the paper down on the chair next to him as the tea and strudel arrived. He noticed that the girl had been glancing at the back page of the paper as he was reading.

"Excuse me. I noticed you were interested in something on the back page of the paper. I am finished with it - not much news of interest to me today. Here, please feel free."

"Oh, thank you. I didn't realize it was so obvious that I was trying to read something while you were doing so. It was rude of me. I am sorry."

*American,* thought Lucas. "No problem. My name is Lucas, by the way. I noticed you were into your map. I'm not from here, but can I help you with something?"

"Well, not really. I'm here on a search for records of some ancestors. I will be going to Prague for the same purpose. I wanted to rent a car for the trip and was looking at various ways to get there from here. I'm not too sure about being alone in a car in the middle of Central Europe, though. I may end up taking the train. In any case, I thank you for your offer, but I think I will be OK. And my name is Caroline. Caroline Weber."

"And, if I may ask, where are you from, Caroline Weber? Somewhere in the heartland of America, I surmise," replied Lucas with a warm smile. Apart from being quite attractive and with somewhat of an athletic look, probably 22 or 23 years old, thought Lucas, she had a pleasant smile and was responsive to his interest in conversation. Direct. American girls are usually like that. Just like Elaine.

"From a small town in Kansas. Westmoreland - a small dot on the map. Farming country. And where are you from? I notice a bit of a British accent."

"I am actually half German and half English. I grew up in London, am living there temporarily now after having lived in your own Washington, D.C. for a few years. I am here in Vienna applying for a job with an international economic development agency."

They smiled at each other, with each appearing to search for something to say.

"So, now that we know why each other is here and where we are from, what else do we talk about?" laughed Lucas.

"Maybe about the best way for me to get to Prague."

Lucas responded "My advice is to take the train. I haven't been there, but the Czech Republic is not far out of their dark 40 years of Communist rule and I am not sure it is wise for a woman to travel there in a car alone."

"Probably a wise thing. I wanted to see many of the towns and historic sites between here and Prague but I think you are right."

After an awkward moment finishing their coffee and tea, Caroline said "Well, it has been nice meeting you. I must be going, though. I have a bit of a walk to make to my hotel." She signaled the waiter for her check and Lucas did the same. When they had paid, Lucas asked her where she was going. He did not want the encounter to end just like that. "My hotel is just off MarianhilferStrasse. About a forty minute walk."

"Oh, I am going in that direction as well (his hotel was nowhere near there - it was just down the street). I can walk you at least part of the way. How about it?"

"Yes, you could." She gave Lucas a big smile as they walked out of the Cafe Griensteidl.

An hour later, after lingering in front of and in a half-dozen or more shops and boutiques on their way up the popular shopping street, they arrived at the door of her hotel.

"Caroline, I would like to see you again. You mentioned you are not leaving for Prague until Tuesday. Could we do something together tomorrow? How about a tour of the Hofburg Palace together - I noticed there are tours of the place leaving every hour? We could maybe have dinner afterwards."

"I think we could. I have already taken a tour of the Hofburg but I would love to do it again. There is so much to see there."

"At the cafe 2 PM tomorrow?"

"Yes, very good," replied Caroline and turned and entered the hotel while waving back to Lucas as she went through the revolving door.

Lucas spent the next half hour walking back to his hotel, wondering where the relationship with this girl would take him. She is lovely...and lively. I could like her a lot, he thought as he wondered what he was going to do for dinner. Idiot! Why didn't you ask her to dinner tonight?

Lucas and Caroline spent the next afternoon touring the Hofburg. They visited the Imperial butterfly house with butterflies settling on their shoulders, heads and hands as they walked through the glassed-in arboretum. They stopped for ice cream on Stephensplatz, talking all the time and ending up for dinner at the elegant Palmenhaus im Burggarten restaurant facing the Palace.

"Saturday night in Vienna. How nice," said a smiling Lucas as they sat down to dinner. The two of them spent the rest of the evening talking about the most recent happenings in their lives.

Caroline was fascinated by Lucas' account of the Singapore affair which led to a discussion of his grandfather, the family history on the German side, the period of his youth in London and his work in international development. Lucas in turn was interested in this engaging, energetic American girl who was rapidly making him forget about Elaine. He appreciated her quest for truth about her own roots and how far she was willing to go in that. They had agreed earlier in the evening to attend the rock concert that was heavily publicized throughout Vienna, but the time flew by and at 11, their waiter was making signs it was time to close up. The realization of what time it was took them by surprise. They decided it was far too late to go over to the concert, so Lucas offered to walk Caroline to her hotel. It was a warm evening, they took their time and when they arrived, Lucas kissed Caroline on the cheek and said goodnight. They agreed to meet Monday after Caroline's meeting with her researcher.

On Monday, Caroline met with the Viennese researcher at the archives office. She provided a verbal overview of what she had discovered after handing Caroline the two page typewritten report.

"Fraulein Weber, there were two Thomas Webers that I was able to find who lived in Vienna in the 1860's. One was a cobbler who was born in Linz, had eight children, and died in Vienna in 1893, which disqualifies him from being who you are looking for."

"The other Thomas Weber, through information gleaned from a Vienna newspaper article in 1870, was a merchant banker. This article said he had come from Bohemia in 1862, acquiring in 1863 a share in a banking syndicate that had an office at the Wiener Borse, the stock exchange. You should know that the Wiener Borse was the one that crashed in 1873, sending Austria and Europe into prolonged economic troubles."

"There is more. Through the property records of the time, I discovered that this Thomas Weber owned a home in Meidling, a suburb of Vienna and that he was a member of the Catholic church in nearby Atzgersdorf. I managed to get access to the archives of that church and found that Herr Weber was born in Bohemia, but without listing exactly where. There was no record of marriage or births of children."

Caroline concluded that this Thomas Weber was more than likely her great-great-grandfather. "Thank you, Madame. What you have uncovered provides the basis for where I go next in all of this. On to Bohemia. I knew the Webers originated from there, but I didn't know anything about the Vienna connection. I understand the basics of that now. A banker. Made a lot of money, it seems, and left for America before the crash." She thanked the Austrian lady, paid her fee and joined the young Englishman she was getting increasingly interested in at the cafe next to the Hofburg Palace.

"Well, how did it go?" asked Lucas as Caroline sat down, letting out a great sigh as she came in from the hot afternoon.

"It went great. I now know where my Weber ancestor got the money to buy all the land he owned in Kansas. He was a banker, for God's sake!"

"A banker? And he moved to rural Kansas - Indian country? Doesn't sound right."

"Well, I pretty much know why. At least why he ceased to be a banker. The great Vienna Crash of 1873 and the widespread speculation running up to it. The Vienna stock market crashed in May of that year. Looks like he avoided getting caught up in it, though. The records back in Kansas say he arrived in New York in early April, a month before the Crash. He got out; probably sold off to his partners or whatever. But, I don't really understand why he ended up in Kansas. I would have thought his banking background would find him in New York or Philadelphia."

"Caroline, as I remember it, the Vienna Crash rippled through Europe and the troubles found their way to America. The banking system in the United States was shaken; many banks failed. Your ancestor maybe wanted no part of being a banker anymore. From what you tell me, it looks like he wanted to be a landowner and do something else. And Kansas had a lot of land for people to buy."

"Yes, I learned about the Crash and the similar troubles in America at the time in my research before I arrived here. So, my ancestor was a banker and a wealthy one at that. Now I have to figure out the Bohemian part of it. I have to start somewhere up there. I have an address for the central archives office. It is in Prague, but there is another one in Plzen. The one in Plzen has a centralized archive of the parish records of births, marriages and deaths of all the Catholic churches in the western part of Bohemia. The Prague archives is a place to start, but I wonder how far my English will get me. You speak German; maybe that would help."

Caroline then looked at Lucas, and said with a mildly pleading tone, "Will you come with me to Prague, my dear English-German friend?"

"Yes, I will. I would love to. I could stand to learn a bit about Bohemia myself. I would be glad to be your bodyguard on the back roads of Bohemia," Lucas replied with a big smile on his face, wondering how the sleeping arrangements would go from then on, but giving no indication to Caroline that the question was on his mind. In any case, he thought, I have nothing else better to do. Word on the UNIDO job would only be coming in two weeks time or longer. I can think of no better way to spend the next week than with this attractive, energetic young woman in front of me. Caroline Weber, here we go.

# Chapter 11

**Marseille, May 1998**

Claudia answered the call at the office. It was Madame Joly, her mother's friend and neighbor in St-Remy.

"Claudia, your mother is not well. She has had a stroke. You must come. She is in the hospital in St-Remy. It is where I am calling from."

"What happened, Madame?"

"I went over this morning to bring her some tulip bulbs. A little after 9. I knocked on the door. There was no answer but your mother's car was in its usual place. She was always up at that hour and always answered the door when I came over. She would usually cry out for me to enter as the door was rarely locked then. I knocked again, and again. After getting no response, I walked around to the back. I looked in the kitchen window and saw your mother lying on the floor. The back door was not locked. I found her unconscious and immediately called the *Service d'Aide* from her telephone. She was breathing, but not responding to me at all. The ambulance came. I fetched my car and followed them to the hospital. She opened her eyes in the emergency area as I arrived but I don't think she recognized me. A few minutes ago, the doctor told me she had a stroke. She is paralyzed on her left side and cannot speak. Her heart beat is irregular. They fear that she may be going. The hospital needs to speak with a family member. Can you speak with the hospital people here? The lady next to me needs to speak with you or with monsieur Brandt."

"Of course. Pass the phone to the lady."

Claudia knew this moment would come. Although her mother was only 74, not really that old for her generation, she had had bouts of depression for years. She neglected herself, reclusing in the house for weeks at a time, as well as showing signs of dementia. From a once stunningly beautiful woman who turned heads of men on the street well into her fifties, she had become a frail wisp of a figure, dieting and fasting, often excessively, as part of her adherence to an obscure Indian sect that preached of fasting and meditation. She had been surprised a few years earlier when she realized her mother had abandoned her Catholic faith. It was something that had been an essential part of her life. Apart from Madame Joly, she had few friends. There was one from her schooldays, Ingrid, who lived in Vienna and would visit her from time to time. They would speak two or three times a year, but Claudia was not sure there had been a contact between the two recently. Her brother Karl visited their mother regularly. Georg was in South America; had been there for years and communicated infrequently. Her other brother Richard would come to St-Remy with his wife for a weekend every summer and did his best to maintain a warm relationship. Isabel wanted nothing to do with their father, however, and had refused his entreaties to visit her and the house in St-Remy for years.

"Madame, I am Isabel Brandt's daughter. I understand her condition is not good."

"You are correct, Madame. Your mother has had a stroke and has some degree of paralysis. We suspect she has some brain damage. She is extremely dehydrated as well and on the verge of kidney failure. You or someone else from the immediate family must come here and as quickly as possible. If your mother goes into a coma, we will need authority to deal with her condition as it evolves."

"I understand. My brother Karl is a doctor. I will have him call you to discuss her condition, if you don't mind. I am in Marseille now and will be leaving for St-Remy within the hour. I suspect my brother will also. What is the telephone number there?"

Karl knew right away from his discussion with the emergency room doctor that the end was near. He called Claudia and they agreed to meet in St-Remy by mid-afternoon. He then called his father and brother Richard with the news. He placed a call to the number he had for Georg in Buenos Aires and left a message, realizing it was 5:30 in the morning local time at his brother's office. Erik and Richard immediately made plans to travel to St-Remy. Both would be able to make it to the hospital sometime that evening.

Isabel Brandt never regained consciousness and died in the early morning hours of the following day. Her husband and three of her four children were by her side. Her eldest son did not make it in time.

---

The funeral and burial was in Gebenbach, the village in Bavaria where Isabel was born and grew up. She was buried alongside the graves of her parents and a brother who had died in childhood.

After the funeral and burial, Erik gathered his three sons and daughter in a small meeting room at the village inn where they were all staying. They would have dinner with spouses and other members of the family later that evening.

"Your mother had no will, as far as I can tell," he said. "I have spoken to the local solicitor she had employed on occasion in St-Remy. He is not aware of any will being filed by her. Claudia, do you know of one? Did your mother ever mention she had written one?"

"No. Nothing of the sort. I believe you are right, Father."

Erik continued. "Your mother and I have a *communauté de biens* according to French law. Whatever we had as a couple would revert to the ownership of the surviving member upon one of our deaths, unless there was a will that declared otherwise.

94

Consequently, it appears that everything we had together at the time of our separation reverts to me. That being said, I wish to explain to you here how I plan to dispose of the family possessions in the short term as well as upon my death. I am getting on, at 81 years, and this discussion with you is timely."

"As you know, I have owned and still own a number of properties that have considerable value today. There is the villa in St-Remy, the apartment in Bonn, a house outside of Nuremberg that is rented, a house in Munich that is rented as well and the island property off the Italian coast, where I plan to stay the rest of my years. This should not be a surprise to you."

Erik went on. "I have decided to dispose of the properties under optimal market conditions in due course and place the proceeds in trust funds for each of you, accessible upon my death. My lawyer has done this in a fashion that will minimize estate taxes. Furthermore, your mother inherited a small amount of money and a house here in this village when her parents, your grandparents, died in the early 1980's. Upon the death of her mother, she sold the house that turned out to have a mortgage on it, leaving a modest net value which we put into a savings account. Your mother had hoped to have a sizable inheritance from her own parents but that was not the case. Whatever, it made little difference in the end. I have always provided for your mother and I hope you realize that."

Erik was on the verge of relating to his children how he had come to have the Brandt properties in the first place, but caught himself. Germans, even the ones of the generation of his children, were accustomed to refraining from enquiring too deeply into family histories. The Nazi era had left scars that would be felt through many succeeding generations. People shied away from asking too many questions. Isabel knew everything, however, including about his brother. He didn't know if she had spoken of it to Claudia or any of his sons. He hoped not. He doubted she had. He would have sensed it.

Karl was the first to speak. "Father, are you sure you want to sell the property in St-Remy? Perhaps one of us would like to have it. It is not the case for me. But Claudia? Richard?"

Claudia was quick to respond. "I do not have fond memories of St-Remy. I have thought of it, but I would prefer to have the money from my share of the proceeds. André and I have our own plans and needs. In any case, we would have to buy out the rest of you if we wanted the villa. Right?"

Erik replied that, "Yes, anyone of you wanting to own alone any of the properties would have to buy out the interests of the others."

"As I thought," said Claudia. "André and I would prefer to have the money from the sale. The island property could perhaps be something else. In any case, as I understand it, Father, it will not be for sale as long as you are alive."

"Georg, Richard, Karl, do you have any objections to my plans for the disposition of the assets?"

Each replied that they did not.

It occurred to Claudia that none of them had any great need for money or for additional properties over and above what they already had. Each was doing well in their respective careers. It was not the case for her.

---

Erik made plans to go to the villa in St-Remy, but had to return to the island after the funeral to attend to some matters that could not wait. He needed to see what papers Isabel had. He was particularly concerned about whatever diaries he suspected she had kept. He had broached the subject of diaries before with Isabel; she always said she did not keep one. He had suspected otherwise over the years, but refrained from pressing the subject. The identities of his family, of his brother in particular, and the truth of Claudia's real parentage were of concern to him. If any of that information fell into the hands of his children and particularly of Claudia, it would lead to a family crisis and certain confrontations with her that he wanted to avoid at all costs. It could destroy the relative peace he had with her and her husband and turn her life as well as his own inside out. Erik returned to the island, looked after the matters requiring his attention, then two days later drove to St-Remy. He would place the management of the property in the hands of an estate agent while he was there as well. For the moment, he needed to find whatever papers Isabel had in her possession.

He did not know and would not know it for some time, however, that Claudia had been there before him. From

Gebenbach, she had driven to St-Remy before going on to Marseille. In the back of a closet off her mother's bedroom, she discovered a small filing cabinet piled high with folded sweaters and hid from view by a long rack of clothing. In the back of the top drawer, she found four volumes of a diary that her mother had kept, with intermittent entries, for over thirty years. The first entry was dated the 10th of June, 1965, the day after she had arrived with Erik to take possession of the villa in St-Remy. The last entry was two years previous, the day after Christmas 1995. Claudia spent the following three hours reading details of her mother's life she knew nothing about, of the real identity of her father and the fact that he had a twin brother who was a Nazi, causing him to change his name, and who, she rapidly discovered through the devastating discovery of her mother's affair, was not her true father. She was the biological daughter of an Austrian stage actor and scion of one of the wealthiest families of Austria and Bohemia.

Claudia's life, her self-identity, the relative peace of mind she had despite the financial and marital difficulties she and André had over the years, would not be the same from that moment forward. She took the diaries, left everything else she had come across in place, and drove to Marseille. She was not sure what she was going to do. The relationship with her father would not, could not be the same, even if it had been strained over the years to begin with. She realized why. Her father never regarded her as his daughter. It was because she was not his daughter and he had known it all along.

---

"What? Your father is not your real father?" asked André as he looked at her across the table.

"Yes. From my mother's diary. I didn't know she kept one. I went by the house on the way back after the funeral. I came across it in a file cabinet tucked away in the back of her closet. I can't believe this. My mother kept the identity of my true father from me all these years. I understand a lot of things now. Why she and father had grown so far apart. And on and on......This really upsets me. It changes things. Changes everything." She then told André what she had found regarding her parentage.

"Wait a minute. Let's go over this," said André. "You say your mother had a fling during a trip to visit a friend in Vienna in 1967. She meets a young man. They have an affair. She becomes pregnant but before she learns of her pregnancy, the young man kills himself in a car accident. When she learns of her pregnancy, she tells Erik. Erik tells her he will take you, the child, as his own. He also tells your mother the young man is most likely the nephew of a friend of his from university days, and a member of one of the wealthiest families of Bohemia and Austria. She learns a few days later through an article in a Paris newspaper that this is the case. Your real father is a Cobourg-Strauss. And Erik Brandt, your erstwhile father, has known this all along. Well, this is all very interesting."

"There is something else, André," continued Claudia.

"My so-called erstwhile father Erik Brandt's real name is Erik Bendt. He had his named changed when he was twenty in 1937 to avoid being identified as the brother of a man who had become a Nazi and was on his way to becoming a leading figure in the party. He moved to Switzerland, took up Swiss citizenship as his mother had been born Swiss and then later renewed his German citizenship after the war in order to be able to work in the diplomatic service of postwar Germany. My mother related in her diary how my father had sought to eradicate any mention of the name of Bendt in his affairs and records over the years."

How truly interesting, thought André.

"Claudia, what was it you told me on the phone about the intentions of your father regarding the disposition of the family property? All of you would share in the proceeds of the sale of properties that would be disposed of based on optimal market conditions?"

"Yes, André, that was it. Full shares for everyone, but it may take a while."

André did not say anything else, but slowly began to mull an idea to have an earlier disposition of property than Erik Brandt would prefer. He needed money, lots of it, and could not wait years. His lawyers were running out of options to keep his creditors at bay. As well, there were his own cousins who were after him. His wife may have just given him a way to solve his problems.

"Does your father know you have this stuff - the diaries?"

"Well, no, I got there first. I am pretty sure he does not know of the diaries to begin with, let alone the fact I have them. I did not take anything else from the house. I did not want him to know I had been there. No one saw me, as far as I can tell. I left everything else as it was."

**Two months later:**

Claudia was livid. "The son-of-a bitch," she said to herself He does have a woman in Paris. *Le chien.*

That morning, she had decided to do some cleaning in André's office while he was away in Paris on a business trip. He had told her it was to close a deal on a big sale to a chain of upscale teen clothing. Behind the desk was one of his briefcases, one of the three he had left at the office. As Claudia lifted it, the lid of the briefcase opened and an envelope dropped out. The envelope was from an address in Paris, addressed to André in elegant long-hand, care of a post office box in Marseille, postmarked a month before. Claudia opened the envelope, and saw what she had sensed for a long time. He was doing it again. A woman named Dany, who said she had enjoyed the relationship which had given her great pleasure. She was asking for help, and inferring it was not the first time - '*comme autrefois*'. "The son of a bitch."

As Claudia sat at André's desk, she reflected on where her life was at. Ten years now with André. He cheats on me. Just like the time four years ago. Probably always has had someone. He's even giving her money. Daddy was right about him. How did I get into this? As if she hadn't had that thought before. She knew why, but she had always run from it.

Security. My life was a mess when I met André. It was a release. It was a way to get away from living with Mama; to move on from relationships with men who only wanted to take me to bed. Freedom from Daddy.....from doing what he wanted me to do. *Mais merde*.....Stuck with a cheating husband who has deals all over the place that don't work out; who cheats Peter to pay Paul. It never ends. I don't even know the extent of it. A husband who wants no children.....doesn't even want to talk about it. And two abortions now. *Merde!*

Why do I put up with this? She knew the answer. It was because she had no other valid option. It had been the case for years and she knew it. They had had some serious rows. She had left André twice. The first time, five years into their marriage, she had caught him in a cafe in Tropez with a woman. Tête à tête, holding hands. She made a row. Flipped. Took a glass of wine from the table, threw it at them, walked out, took her clothes from the apartment and drove to St-Remy.

Claudia's mind turned to that particular day. When she arrived at the villa, Isabel was in the garden at the back. She had not seen her mother for three or four months

*"Bonjour, maman."* Her mother turned, looked at Claudia, and replied "Where did you go?" At that moment, Claudia realized that her mother, at only 70 years of age, was showing

signs of dementia. She remembered her mother quickly correcting herself. "Oh, what am I talking about? You are back? What brings you? Where is André?"

"Mother, I am back for awhile. Taking another break. André is very busy."

Claudia spent the following two weeks with her mother. She knew she couldn't stay forever. It was clear Isabel was having memory lapses and someone would have to keep a close watch on her. She went to see the neighbor, Madame Joly. They agreed to speak often. The lady would check on her mother every day. The two had enjoyed afternoon tea for years, in any case.

André called her every day. Begged her to come back. Said he would make it up to her. The affair was over. Said he loved her, that he would help her start a business to make up for everything. She would not have to work at the company anymore. She went back.

The little shop. It was great, she thought. Lovely, little boutique for women in the old part. It did well and was profitable almost from day one. André had put up the money for it in exchange for living up to the promise to Claudia but had insisted on having signing authority for the boutique's bank account. One day he raided the account and told Claudia they had to close the boutique, at least temporarily.

"André, how could you do this? I have regular customers. I have a business. I have a lease on the space. I have put everything into it. How could you?"

She remembered the scene as if it were yesterday. That was it. What a shit! Needed the money, he said. She left and went to her mother's again. Isabel got upset. Argued with Claudia about her life just about every day. Claudia argued back. Like two cats, she recalled. At other times, Isabel was silent, off in her own world, a depressing spectacle. It was not an enjoyable time for Claudia. She knew she had to find another solution. She couldn't stay there. Her mother was better off with Madame Joly looking after her.

Anne, a friend who lived outside Marseille, offered to have her live with her for awhile. It lasted for a few weeks but was far from being an ideal solution. She had no money, no job. André controlled everything. There was no way she was going to ask her father for help. It would only be vindicating his disgust with her relationship with André. It was not long after her first abortion. He had insisted. "No children," he said. "Not part of the deal, Claudia."

André of course knew where she was. He showed up one day after she had been there a week; came back almost every day. Talked her into coming back; said he would make it up to her, again, that he loved her. The boutique opened up again a few weeks later, but the damage was done. She never managed to regain the clientele and the bank would not provide a line of credit, no doubt influenced by André's less than stellar reputation in the local banking community. She closed the boutique at the end of the lease a few months later.

My life is a mess, she thought At thirty years of age, Claudia Brandt was a beautiful woman. She turned men's heads on the street, as she had ever since she was fifteen. Men gravitated to her. She resisted the advances. Maybe I should be more accommodating, she thought. Do unto him as he has been doing unto me. Next time an attractive man makes a pass at me, I just may respond.

André, what a shit he is. Gone all the time. Secrets about everything. Supposedly doing great deals with people in the Middle East, in Asia. Then the real estate stuff and whatever else with the Italian side of the family that he doesn't want to talk to me about. The restaurant he had with Gino gone bust. He probably cheated Gino in the process. They were no longer friends. That was for sure. She and André had run into Gino in a cafe a few months previous and a big argument ensued.

This is it, she thought. Le divorce. I am just going to have to do it. Can't go on this way anymore. But, the nagging thought came back. Where will I go? She decided to go out, clear her head. She went to a café down by the wharf to have an espresso and think.

As thoughts were going through her head, Claudia's attention was drawn to a familiar face that was walking towards the cafe from across the street. Why, it's Marco's wife, Antonia.

Marco Scalia was one of André's cousins from his mother's side who lived in Genoa. André never wanted to talk very much about the Italian side of his family. Nevertheless, they had gone to Genoa a couple of times over the past few years, once for a big family dinner and another for the funeral of an aunt. She remembered Antonia, although it had been years since she had seen her. At that same instant, the attractive dark-haired woman crossing the street recognized Claudia. Her eyes widened and a broad smile crossed her face. She quickly moved towards the cafe.

"Claudia, what a pleasant surprise. How are you?" as she came down the aisle.

"I am fine, Antonia. Very nice to see you. What brings you to Marseille? But before answering that, please sit down. Can you join me for a coffee?"

"I would be glad to. So good to see you."

After a few pleasantries and the ordering of a coffee for the newcomer to the table, Antonia opened up. "Claudia, Marco and I are no longer together. I left him three weeks ago, by the way just after the last time André had been at the house. My daughter and I are living with my cousin not far from here."

This surprised Claudia on more than one count. Antonia's admission of her separation was one but the second one was the one that really struck. "André was at your house in Genoa three weeks ago?"

"You didn't know, Claudia? It was the third, maybe the fourth time over the last few weeks. One other time at our house. The other times at Marco's office. Big arguments between the two of them. You didn't know? André didn't tell you?"

"No, Antonia, I'm afraid he didn't. I have no idea. What was this about?"

"Claudia, it is about time you know some things about the relationship between Marco and André. I suspect that André has not told you about their difficult relationship over the past few months. It has contributed to my decision to leave Marco. My husband, his brother, and I regret to say, a few other male members of the family are rough businessmen and there are people in Genoa who would say they are mafia. They don't do business in a very nice way. Marco is being very difficult with André. He has not been nice. On the other hand, you must know that André has contributed to the difficulties he has with his cousin."

Antonia went on. "There is a history to it. You must know that André's mother and Marco's father were sister and brother and were very close when growing up. Apparently, when André's mother married Joseph Gralla, the family objected. They suspected Joseph was Jewish. No one ever really determined if that was the case. He was certainly not Italian, though, and this caused a rift in the family. Nevertheless, André stayed in touch with the Scalias over the years, even after his mother died when he was a boy. But they - I mean André and Marco and his brother Luca - had never done business before. They used to hang around together when they were younger, but had never done any business together. Not until sometime last year."

Claudia was certain she was about to learn things that would upset her, but that would also allow her to understand what her husband was up to. As Antonia said, it was about time. "Tell me, Antonia. What happened? I need to know."

"André came to Marco sometime last year to ask him for a loan. For a lot of money; something like 400 hundred thousand Euros. He said he needed it to pay off a debt. It had something to do with the failure of a restaurant he owned. Said he could pay it back within six months. He would sell the property where the restaurant was. Marco was a real shit, though. He's rough. Cousin or no cousin. He said he would loan André the money but he would have to sell the property faster than that. The loan needed to be repaid within 90 days. I only found out about all this from Luca's wife a few weeks ago. Luca had explained everything to her, describing how their cousin André had lied about the need for money from the boys and had lied about his ability to repay it."

Claudia said, "Go on. What happened?" She was beginning to understand why André had raided every source of cash he could get his hands on. He had to repay his cousin.

"Well, when the ninety days were up, Marco called André and told him he had to pay up. André told him he couldn't. He said he hadn't sold the restaurant property yet. Marco in the meantime had learned that André was not even the owner of the property. It was owned by his partner in the restaurant."

Gino, thought Claudia.

"Marco then apparently confronted André with this, saying that he had been lied to. He told André that he had to come up with the money and it had to be done quickly and hung up. According to Luca, Marco was furious that he had been lied to by his cousin."

Antonia continued, while finishing her espresso. "A couple of weeks later, André showed up at our house. He and Marco went into the living room. I stayed away in the kitchen. I could hear them shouting, though. I only learned later that André had brought something like seventy-five thousand Euros to help pay off the debt. This upset Marco. He threw the money at André and told him to come back with it all. André left the money on the floor, turned, and walked past me in the kitchen and out the back to his car."

"And?" asked Claudia.

"Marco knows something about André and decided to blackmail him. I told you, the Scalia boys are rough. It is the blackmail thing that I confronted Marco with that eventually led to my leaving him. There were other reasons. It all added up. Marco has a mistress - a twenty year old university student he keeps an apartment for. I found out about it about the same time as I became aware of the blackmail thing. Frankly, a twenty year old! The last straw."

"Blackmail? Blackmail about what?" asked Claudia.

"I don't know. Something that could get André into trouble with the authorities. Something he did years ago that Marco knew about."

Claudia did not know what to make of what she was hearing. What could it be? What else has he kept from me?

She looked at Antonia and decided to change the focus of the discussion. It was painful enough already. "What about you now, and your daughter, Antonia? Marco accepting this?"

"Marco doesn't care. He can have all the women he wants. I sent him a note saying I expected nothing from him. That I would get along just fine. We had been together twelve years. It was long enough. He could have all the access he wanted to his daughter and all the women he wanted with no troubles from me. I have heard nothing back. I have a new job with a company here in Marseille. I have a degree in marketing from my university days that has become handy. Which reminds me. I have to go. Need to get back to the office. I have only been there a week."

Antonia looked at Claudia as she rose from the table. "I hope I haven't disturbed you too much with all this, Claudia. I just think you should know. I do want to see you again, however." She scribbled something on a piece of paper she had taken from her purse. "Here is my number at the office. Call me. Maybe next time we can talk about more pleasant things."

"This has told me a lot," a stunned Claudia blurted out. "I am glad we met. Thank you, Antonia. We will stay in touch. All the best," said Claudia as she smiled weakly while Antonia leaned over, kissed her on both cheeks, turned, and went on her way down the street.

Claudia sat back in the chair, tilted her head back and looked off into the bay with a blank stare. How did I get myself into this?

After a few moments, the question became something else. How do I get myself out of this?

**Marseille, two weeks later:**

André and Claudia were to meet at the restaurant down the street from the Hotel de Ville. She had been at her friend's house for a week. Over the past few days, André had decided that the best way to solve his problems was to repair his relationship with his wife. He actually did love her. None of the mistresses and the women he had came close to Claudia for living up to his dream of the woman of his life, for sex, for being beautiful, for being loving when she felt like it. She was also great for business. Whatever success they had had with their businesses over the years, it was in the ones Claudia had a hand in. If she divorced him, which she had threatened to do, particularly since she discovered the letter from the girl in Paris, he would lose everything. The trophy wife, the sex and the warmth on the good days, the business help, and, in the end, the most important source of financial survival for him, her inheritance from the old man. Can't afford to lose that. Have to patch it up. She wants a child. We'll make a child if that what keeps her.

André arrived early and beckoned Claudia to sit when she arrived a few minutes later. He quickly began what he had to say, "Claudia, I am a real shit to you. You probably won't accept this, but I am sorry." He looked her in the eye and received a skeptical return gaze. After a short pause, he leaned forward and continued, "I have actually loved you from the day I first saw you. It's true. Despite the affairs. Despite the untruths and whatever I have held back from you. I love you and have always loved you. I have done stupid things in business and many stupid things in life.....I am sorry. Truly sorry. Can we patch things back together? Is it possible?"

André then put up his hand as he observed the doubt in her expression. "But before you answer, and I can see in your eyes your distrust of what I am saying, I have some things to tell you. You deserve to know these things. I do my mea culpa. With this, maybe you will forgive me."

André proceeded to tell her everything, or almost everything. He admitted to the affairs. Told her about the deals. The drug money running through the restaurant. It was why he and Gino had split. Gino wanted no part of the drug stuff. André had been using the restaurant as a drop for the cocaine. Easy money. Beat selling t-shirts. The operation lasted four months; "Lucky to get away with not being caught." The only really criminal thing he had ever done, he told her. The dumbest thing as well. Had cheated some people in the past, but it was business, not criminal. He proceeded to explain that the cocaine was kept in a cabinet in the back storage room. Had a lot of it there and he owed the supplier a lot of money on it. "Louis, the waiter at the restaurant, you remember him?  He was the runner. Gino didn't know about it. I was going to stop the operation; had made enough money off of it to take care of what I owed on the apartments in St. Paul. Well, before I could unload the last shipment, which was the biggest I had taken on, Louis one day took off with it all and disappeared. Million Euros worth on the street. I still had to pay the supplier. I went to Marco to get a loan. I was scared. But I saw no other option. Marco insisted on 90 days. I had no choice but to say yes. The supplier was after me. A Moroccan guy. Dangerous. Threatened to kill me."

Claudia sat back, but said nothing. A lot of this she already knew from Antonia, but elected to remain silent. She figured there was more to come, and there was.

André fidgeted with the glass in front of him, then continued, "Claudia, maybe this will explain some things. I am telling you everything, but I am not done. Cousin Marco threatened to blackmail me. My own cousin. He threatened me a few months ago to inform the police of my so-called drug-running. I had brought 75,000 Euros to him as a first payment. He threw it on the floor. Said it was not good enough. "Work it out, André. Find a way. You lied to me. Nobody lies to me, least of all people in my own family." A month or so later, he called me - said he knew where Louis the waiter was; could lead the police to him - it would lead back to me. I told him I would cover everything, but it would take time." André purposely omitted that the real blackmail was about the incident with the Romanian sailor years before. He would never tell Claudia about that. "A couple of days later, I withdrew 50,000 Euros from the restaurant bank account and brought it to him. Caused the break-up with Gino. Now you know why on that score. I didn't know where else to go to get Marco to back off. He wasn't there so I left it with Luca, who was at the house. Antonia wasn't there either. Heard nothing for awhile. I started to get worried about what he may be up to. The blackmail thing was still out there. Three weeks ago, I called him; said we needed to talk. We met and, in the end, I managed to get him to back off for a few months. He said he would wait for another year for the balance but said I would have to pay him interest - 3% per month, compounded. Said it would normally be 10% per month, but I was family, so he would be generous." André was lying. No special deal from Marco - the interest would be 10% per month, which would easily triple the final amount owed, if not more, by the time it was paid off.

André paused to take a drink of water, then continued, as Claudia said nothing. "So, I bought some time, but I will have to take care of it in the end. The clothing deals I went to Paris for will hopefully generate enough profit to reduce what I owe him, although I am not sure it will be good enough for all of it." The contrite supplicant trying to convince his skeptical wife to stick with him purposely neglected to say that there was little prospect in clearing the debt that way. Something else would have to be found and he saw little else but the triggering of the inheritance from her father.

"How much will that be in the end, André?"

"Close to 500,000 Euros." He lied. It would be well over a million and counting. After a little over eight months, with 10% interest per month compounded, he already owed Marco close to 800,000 Euros. Interim payments were not even covering accumulating monthly interest.

André quickly moved to counter the doubt expressed in Claudia's expression, "I should be able to cover it. Marco and I will work it out. It has not been fun. I will never do the drug thing again, Claudia. You must know that. And I don't want to lose you. Can we try to make it work again?"

Claudia responded "I don't know. I have to think. I don't know. *Je ne sais pas.*"

"There is something else, my dear. I think it is time we had a child. I mean that, if you still want one." Claudia was stunned. André had always refused to consider having children. This was new. What? What has gotten into him? A baby....now.....after all the shit he has put me through?

"André, I have to think about all this. All you have done. Your affairs. All the other stuff. I just can't wipe all that away just like that. I need to think. I don't know. I will call you. Right now, I need to go. I will cry if I don't." Claudia rose, went around the table, kissed her still-seated errant husband on the top of the forehead, turned and walked out of the restaurant.

**The next day:**

"Val, we need to get together. I need to talk to you. It's been awhile. Are you free for lunch tomorrow?"

Claudia seemed distressed on the phone. Valerie Poulin was Claudia's best friend in Marseille. "Of course. What is going on, my dear?"

"It's about André and I. I just need to talk about it. Are you free tomorrow?" implored Claudia.

"Sure. Let's meet at the Coquille. See you then," responded Valerie, referring to the bistro on the waterfront they had lunched at frequently over the years.

Claudia was already seated when Valerie arrived for lunch the next day.

"Claudia, my dear, you did not sound very well yesterday, but as usual, you look stunning. Good to see you," Valerie said as the tall blond Claudia Brandt Gralla rose and kissed her best friend on each cheek in the customary French fashion.

"If my looks are great as you believe, my spirit is in flux. I will explain, but in the meantime, glad you are here, Val," said Claudia with a big smile on her face. "Let's have a glass of wine."

After some pleasantries and the ordering of the wine, hearing from the waiter what was special on the menu that day, and the ordering of their usual salads, Claudia began. "André has been cheating on me. *Ça me dégoute.* I found a letter in one of his briefcases from a woman in Paris. More of the same stuff I

116

have confronted him with in the past. I walked out again. Went to stay with Anne two weeks ago."

"Why didn't you call me, Claudia? I hope you know you would have been welcome with Henri and I," said Valerie.

"Of course, I know that, but Anne lives alone and it seemed more convenient for everyone. Anne and I had done this once before, as you will recall. You have your own husband. Anyway, I went to Anne's. André called every day. Wanted me back. Promised to explain things, make up to me. We finally got together two days ago. Quite a meeting it was. As you have probably surmised over the years, André's business affairs have not always been without controversy. He has owed people money and has found all sorts of ways of getting through tough times. He explained everything to me, what the status of his affairs is, the real reason he took the money from the boutique a couple years ago - you remember that - and everything else, as far as I can tell. Anyway, he broke down. Implored that he would change, that he loved me, that he could not imagine living without me. No more affairs, no more ladies in Paris. *Le tout.*"

"Do you believe him?" asked Valerie.

"I don't know. He said something else. That we should have a child. He never, ever said that before. I have difficulty believing him." Claudia paused for a moment, and then continued. "I have never seen him so contrite. Not the same, but. *Je ne sais pas,*" said Claudia as she closed her eyes and shook her head, before gazing into the eyes of her best friend.

"A child, huh?" chuckled a skeptical Valerie across the table. "Typical of a guy who wants back in."

"Val, listen, you know how much I want a child, be a mother, even have more than one. You know how much the abortions affected me. I hated them. He made me." Claudia stopped, paused a few seconds, then continued, "I want a family. I'm no different than other women. I grew up alone. I want more than that. I just don't know about André and his promises."

She went on. "I don't want to live alone, Val. It terrifies me. My mother is gone, my father is in another world - has been for me all my life. My brothers have their own families and are not around to help me - never have been for that matter. If I had a man – somebody else - who I could love and who loved me, it would be different. But I don't. I'm not in the mood for any affairs or games with a Pierre, Jean, Jacques...I had enough of that when I was 19 and 20. I know André. He can be a real shit, but we have had our good moments. I just don't know."

At that moment, the waiter arrived, interrupting the discussion. Over coffee, Valerie brought Claudia back to the subject. "I don't know what to tell you. I fear you may be hurt once again if you go back. But I don't have another solution. All the other avenues appear to be solitary ones. Sleep on it. It has only been two days. Do you love him? Can you love him?"

"Maybe. I have to love myself first, and that is what is difficult."

"Well, my dear, I have to go. Let's talk tomorrow. Call me. Let me pay for the lunch." Valerie rose, went around the table, kissed Claudia on the cheek, then motioned for the waiter as she walked toward the door.

Merde, exclaimed Claudia under her breath. What to do? Alone again. No, no, no, she thought.

Early the next morning, Claudia rose and after a solitary coffee and croissant in Anne's kitchen, called André. They met an hour later and Claudia told him she was coming back. They would work to have a child. They could start that night.

# Chapter 12

## July 1999

The six months since their getting back together had been largely consumed by André's attempts to sort out his business affairs and by their attempted dealings with Claudia's father. André's company had received a big order for clothes, making enough money to keep his cousin at bay. As he had promised, he lavished love and affection on Claudia, surprising her. Two acrimonious meetings with Erik about inheritance and property disposition had taken place, without any tangible result. Erik remained fixed on his plan for disposition of the family properties. In any case, Claudia's attitude towards her father had changed since discovering the diary. The man was not her real father. He had made life miserable for her mother. The bottom line was that she needed her share then, not years from then.

The payments to Marco every month were bleeding them dry. They could ill afford to wait for the trust fund money. Erik would have to die for any of it to come into their hands. At 82, he was still robust and could live many more years.

In the weeks after the reunion with her husband, Claudia learned the full extent of his difficulties, at least what she thought to be the extent of such. Some due to bad luck, others from bad judgment. She learned that an Italian bank that had lent money to his clothing import business to pay for inventory build-up in previous years held a lien on the company building and was threatening to foreclose. Deals with German and French retailers for large quantities of women's silk blouses from Bangladesh had fallen through as the blouses turned out to be of poor quality. The inventory was languishing in the warehouse, with no apparent takers but for small lots - nowhere near what was required to move all of the materiel. The agreement with the Paris-based youth clothing chain was a god-send for keeping them afloat, but it wasn't enough. The Société Générale de France in Marseille had given André six months to repay what he owed for renovations to a restaurant he had supposedly owned that did not exist anymore. Another bank was after André for a delinquent loan it had provided as seed money for the development three years before of a hill-top apartment property outside of St. Paul de Vence that never got built. André had used that loan to pay off a creditor on another deal gone sour the year before. Claudia knew about that one and had been particularly upset about it. She had looked forward to living in the terraced top floor of the building in St. Paul overlooking the bay of Nice.

In the year since her mother's death, André and Claudia had often spoke of the ability to take care of everything, if only

Claudia could succeed in pressuring her father to either will to her the island property or failing that, accelerate the sales of the other properties.

Claudia's reasoning with Erik was that she was the only daughter and deserved a break. The three sons were all well-off and had their own lives. They had no need nor had expressed the desire to have the island property. They rarely visited it to begin with. But André surmised that when it would come to a decision on the matter, none of the boys would readily concede to forego their share of its value. Nevertheless, why not will it to Claudia? He owed it to her - he had neglected her all her life and could wipe out much of the bad feelings about it through such a concession. By stretching the argument a bit, it could be said that the deal would ultimately be fair to all. The value of the other properties had a combined value much greater than the value of the island property and the proceeds of their sale could be arranged to accrue to only the boys if the island property was willed to Claudia.

The two knew it would not be a completely fair deal to her brothers. André was doubtful if the proposal could get very far with Erik, and he was right. At Claudia's first meeting with him on this matter on the island in December, just before Christmas, it had gotten nowhere. This could go on for years, he thought.

At the meeting in December and a second one in March when André was present, Erik announced that he would continue as planned with the disposition of the properties into a common trust fund for all four children and would continue to live on the island in the meantime. He did not want to hear anything more about it.

The last discussion he and Claudia had on the matter was soon after Erik had returned from Singapore on a trip he was reluctant to talk about. Claudia showed up unannounced. She had come with what she thought to be a compelling argument about fairness - she was the only daughter, she was the one who had taken the most care of her mother. The boys had been absent. It was time to rectify the unfairness. She had decided she would not confront her father with the truth of her parentage. That would certainly kill any deal that could be made. The result was similar to the other discussions with one change that was even worse for Claudia and André. Erik told her he wanted now to keep the castle-like villa in the family for the use of present and future generations and have his will changed to reflect that. It would not be disposed of, even at his death. That would leave less money to distribute. Damn, this is even worse, Claudia told herself. She was on the verge of spilling to her erstwhile father everything she knew of her true father, her mother's affair, his real name, everything. Out of anger. Of frustration. She stopped herself. Someday, I will. Not now. I can't. If I really want to upset my life, really upset it, that would do it. André, you are going to have to find another way. And Daddy, someday, we are going to talk about the truth of my existence.

Through all the discussions between Claudia and her father, it had been obvious to her that Erik had seen the hand of André with all of his troubles behind the proposal. He had sources of information in France and he used them to follow André Gralla's affairs. Erik Brandt had no trust whatsoever in the man, deplored the fact his daughter was married to him, and viewed his own plan for the disposition of the properties to be the best way to protect the interests of all of his children, including Claudia.

In the meantime, Erik had no way of knowing that Claudia was aware that he was not her father. He did not find anything resembling a diary in Isabel's possessions. Maybe there was none, he thought.

**August 1999**

"Claudia, let's take a trip," said André over an early morning coffee. "It will do us some good. How about Prague? I have never been there. A week away from Marseille and this heat will do us some good." Lurking in his mind as always was the financial squeeze he was in, which would come to a head with Marco soon enough. Would be good to get away for awhile, he thought.

"*Pourquoi pas,* why not? Never been there either," replied Claudia. Although the thought of her being of somewhat Bohemian descent through her biological father had intrigued her, she had never given much thought to going to Bohemia or Prague, and even less to pursue information on her recently discovered ancestry.

Two mornings later, André and Claudia were on their way.

André had never told Claudia of his Czech Jewish ancestors and of their disappearance in the Holocaust. And he had no intention of telling her anything of it in Prague. It was his secret and it would stay that way.

---

"Claudia, I am not going to walk up that hill to the castle. It is too far up," as they came to the far end of the medieval and wholly pedestrian Charles Bridge. "Let's find a taxi."

"My dear, I am afraid that Prague is all about walking and discovering things around every corner, up every street, down every alley. It's part of being here. Getting up that hill should not be that difficult. It's beautiful. Look up the street. We can take our time." The elegant Hradcany Castle loomed above them in its imposing massive splendor, with the spires of St. Titus Cathedral rising up over the walls that stretched for a full kilometer across the hill above the city.

"Alright, you win. We will walk up to the famous Castle of Prague. But once we get there, I am going to find a cafe terrasse and have a pastis or a beer. I'll wait for you, *mon amour*."

They had spent the day walking around the old city. An hour before, they had traversed the section of the Old Town that was known as the Jewish Quarter. In the centuries and decades before the Second World War, Prague's Jewish population had been sizable and concentrated in an area near the eastern end of the Charles Bridge. André noticed the entrance to the Jewish

Museum and Cemetery. He made a note to visit it before leaving. He would do it alone - perhaps the next morning while Claudia would be shopping. Maybe he could find something about a Maurice Gralla and his family and what happened to them. The tour guide book said there was a list on the walls of the museum of the 77,000 Jews of Bohemia who disappeared into the Holocaust of Europe.

André found a cafe down from the entrance to the castle, but had to settle for a beer. Neither the waiter nor the young bartender knew anything about pastis.

Later that evening, as they were having dinner on the Old Town Square, André asked Claudia if she intended on doing any research on the Cobourg-Strauss family, either while they were in Bohemia or otherwise.

"I would like to, but I would not know where to start. I suppose I would like to know something about them eventually. I am a descendant after all, although I will probably never be able to prove it. All I have is an entry in my mother's diary. I suppose I could contact Ingrid Waller, her friend, who I guess knew all about my mother's affair."

"You don't want to pursue the connection?" intoned André as they were finishing their meal. "You never know. Somebody in the extended family sympathetic to the death of Michael Coburg years ago could perhaps be interested in the existence of a child no one in the family knew he sired."

"André, my dear, how could I prove that I am the child of a Cobourg-Strauss? DNA? Matching along those lines is not very extensive yet. In any case, where would I get a sample of Michael Cobourg-Strauss' DNA? Dig up his grave? I don't think the family would go for that. The former head of the family was an old friend of my father, for God's sake."

"I suppose I should look into it," Claudia sighed. "I know it will just make me more upset than I already am about all this. I am a bastard child, with a mother who never told me anything about who I really am."

Claudia paused, then looked out to the square and the steady procession of people strolling across its wide expanse, then continued with a twinge of anger and impatience with her partner across the table, "Right now, at this moment, André, I am enjoying myself here in Prague, but mainly, all I want is for us to get out of our mess and be able to live normal lives."

The discussion had put Claudia in a bad mood. "The pressure you have wanted me to put on my father to get more out of him has gotten us nowhere. I agreed to do it, yes, perhaps out of revenge against my parents. But it has only further estranged me from the other members of the family. In my view we have no chance of getting money from the estate anytime soon. It makes no sense, in the end, trying to get the island property all to ourselves. My father and brothers will never agree to it. In any case, Father has said no. He even wants the property to stay in the family after his death. Says it is a jewel and should be kept for everyone to be able to use. He would provide for its upkeep for a few years after his death. We are not getting closer to getting the villa and whatever is in the inheritance any time sooner. We are instead getting farther away from it."

She paused a moment, then continued, looking directly into her husband's eyes across the table, "And, by the way, I would like to be a mother some day and soon. I am 31 now and I don't want to wait much longer."

"Claudia, what do you think we have been trying to do for the last half year? We have sex three times a week, for God's sake."

"I know. We will just have to keep at it, I guess."

While Claudia went shopping the next morning, André, after telling her he would find a cafe and some newspapers to fill the time, walked the six blocks from the hotel to the Jewish Museum. Before entering, he took a walk through the walled confines of the cemetery, which for 300 years until the late 1700s, was the only burial ground permitted for the Jews of Prague. Due to the lack of space, people had been buried one on top of another, up to 12 layers deep, according to the pamphlet he took when entering. There were over 10,000 gravestones piled askance, atop or next to dozens of others, protruding in close proximity and at all angles, sitting over the remains of over 100,000 people.

After finding his way through the crooked, meandering lanes of the cemetery, André got to the museum, which contained a variety of belongings, pictures and writings of people, particularly of children, who had been taken away by the Nazis. More importantly for André, however, were the names written on the walls, of the 77,000 Jews deported to Terezin and ultimately to the death camps. Terezin was a small city north of Prague and forever known as the staging ground for the disposition of Jews from Bohemia to their ultimate extermination camp destinations.

It took André Gralla no more than twenty minutes to find the names of his grandfather, Maurice Gralla and his grandmother, Hanna Gersten Gralla. There was no indication where they had been sent to exterminated or when, just their names and where they came from - Pilsen or Plzen in Czech.

On his way towards the museum's exit, André walked by exhibits of artifacts and pictures of the Jewish community before and during the war. Behind glass casings were pictures of children and other people who had disappeared along with their writings and many of their simple possessions. In the last of the glass exhibits in the hallway leading to the exit, there were pictures of German officers and officials. One of them caught his eye. It was of a man with features that were familiar. He got closer. I know this man. I have seen him before, he thought. André read the caption 'Helmut Bendt, Head of the Gestapo, Praha, 1942." The writing below the caption and others of officers and officials in various poses said that these men had been the organizers of the deportation of an estimated 46,000 Czech Jews to Terezin in 1942 and 1943. It also stated that

Helmut Bendt was Prague Gestapo Station Chief from 1941 through 1944.

André's eyes widened as he took a deep breath. Helmut Bendt. I know where I have seen this face. It is the face of Claudia's father. It is the image of him. *Copie conforme.* Yes, Isabel's diary said that Erik's real name was Bendt and that he had changed it to Brandt because of a brother who had joined the Nazis. He looks just like him. This is he. There can be no mistake. My God, the man who deported my grand-parents to their deaths.......the man responsible for the destruction of my family's wealth..... was the brother of my father-in-law......I can't believe this.

His hands were shaking as he left the museum. He walked unsteadily across the street and stopped. After a moment, he relaxed and a faint smile came to his lips. I just may have a solution, he thought. Turning the corner towards the old square and the hotel further on, he wondered if the old man knew this exists.

---

"How was your morning?" asked Claudia as she arrived at the sidewalk cafe where André was relaxing with a Perrier and an espresso.

André had decided he was not going to tell Claudia of his time at the museum. He was not sure he ever would tell her about it. "It proved to be an interesting morning. I walked around, went into a few shops, almost bought a beer mug and a T-shirt with

PRAHA on it in big letters. For a few minutes, I followed the workings of the astrological clock on the City Hall Tower - very interesting - then came back and have been here waiting for you, my dear. How was your shopping?"

"It was wonderful. Such great bargains. I managed to hold myself back, but did find a lovely pair of earrings and bracelet and something for the bedroom, by the way, that I think you will like," with a mischievous smile on her face. She is really serious about having a baby, he thought.

*"Très bien.* Let's have some lunch. We can have it here, then continue our tour of the sights and sounds of Prague this afternoon," as he motioned to the waiter and pulled back a chair for his wife to sit next to him. André was finding himself in a good mood, and understood why. And it had more to do with something other than the prospect of sex with his wife, although that was always a pleasant thought in itself.

André awoke in a sweat. Bad dream. I was there. Middle-aged couple, their home invaded. Nighttime - men in overcoats, pistols drawn, ordering them into a car. Then a boxcar to a place where they were separated, stripped, put into a large room with hundreds of other people. Through the screams of a hundred voices, the woman fainting. My grandparents.

He was there. He was watching it. He could touch the walls of the chamber. The dream ended with the image of a pile of twisted naked bodies being pushed into a pit by gaunt men in rags who then shoveled dirt into the pit until the ground was covered and all traces of the people buried underneath taken from view. He realized it was all from scenes of a film he had seen years before. He would have the nightmare again and again in the weeks that followed.

---

Sometime in the early afternoon two days later, André and Claudia's Peugeot crossed a small red Skoda sedan coming in the other direction just outside the old Bohemian town of Tabor. The occupants of the vehicles paid no attention to the car or the occupants coming from the opposite direction and were oblivious to the fact that their lives would soon cross.

An hour later, Claudia and André stopped for lunch in the castle town of Jindrichuv Hradec and took a tour of the castle before continuing on their way to the Austrian border and the rest of their way home to Marseille. André found very interesting the description by the tour guide of an incident involving the scion of the family who owned the castle at one time being thrown from the window of the premier castle of the realm, which led to some great war hundreds of years before. Defenestration, she called it.

# Chapter 13

**Cesky Krumlov, Southern Bohemia, August 1999**

"This place is awesome, Lucas," observed Caroline as they walked slowly through the narrow streets of the UNESCO World Heritage site.

It was a lovely day with tourists taking in the sites and enjoying a beer or a coffee in the many sidewalk cafes lining the narrow streets of the old town. Lucas and Caroline crossed the river, walked up the steep cobblestoned street and entered the castle where they signed up for a tour which was to soon begin.

The pamphlet read that Cesky Krumlov was founded in the 13th century and was the dominant town of South Bohemia for hundreds of years. It was ruled from the early 1300's to the early 1600's by the Rozmberk (House of Rosenberg) dynasty. After being purchased by the Austrian Emperor Rudolf II, his son, the Emperor Ferdinand II gave the town and castle to another family, who had it for the following one hundred years. From the early

1700's to 1947, over two hundred and twenty five years, it was owned by two other noble families allied with the ruling Austrian Habsburg emperors.

Lucas and Caroline learned in the tour that in 1938 the area was annexed by Nazi Germany as part of the so-called Sudetenland. The town's German-speaking population (according to the guide, 70% of the population in the last pre-war census) was expelled after World War II and the restoration of it to Czechoslovakia. In 1948, the town and the castle were taken over by the state, which had become Communist by that time. The castle fell into disrepair during the Communist era and only after the Velvet Revolution of 1989 had the town and castle begun to be restored to its former beauty. With 300 rooms, the castle was the second largest in the Czech Republic, only after Hradcany Castle of Prague. The tour turned out to be Caroline and Lucas' introduction to Bohemian history. Caroline quickly realized that what she had read in her research in the library of her alma mater back in Kansas was but a glimpse of what she would be learning in towns like Krumlov.

Before leaving, Lucas and Caroline had an early dinner in one of the old town's many inviting outside restaurants. Accompanying their meal with some excellent Czech beer, they sampled the first dish that was advertised in English on the menu - the traditional Czech dish of neck of pork and potato dumplings.

"Heavy stuff, but pretty good, no?" quipped Lucas as they dug into the meal before them.

"Yes, heavy fare, but it is good; almost as good as the pork ribs back home, I might add. The beer, by the way, certainly beats the Budweiser I have from time to time back in Kansas."

"Caroline, the name Budweiser actually comes from here. There is a Czech Budweiser brewery - I saw a sign for it on the street here - that has most probably nothing to do with the Budweiser beer of the Anheuser Busch brewery back in America."

"Lucas, have you noticed there is no reference to German or the German language here?" asked Caroline as they were finishing their early dinner. "Nothing in German anywhere, although we are only a few miles from the Austrian border and the place being of majority German-speaking population for centuries."

"The Nazis caused it all. My grandfather lived through that period, before and during the war. He decided to escape and went to Switzerland. There are things in his past that he has not wanted to talk about. As recently as six weeks ago in Singapore after my release, I almost got him to speak about it, but he changed the subject. Thinking about it, I will be seeing him next week and I am going to try to get him to talk about it. It may be my last chance. He's 82."

After a reflective pause, Lucas continued. "The people here, as those in Poland and Russia and most of the rest of Europe, suffered terribly during that period. No one was kind to ethnic Germans after the war. Vengeance and retribution for the sins of the Nazis. I am sure we will see throughout our visit the extent to which the German influence and heritage has been erased. That being said, I overheard a lot of German being spoken today. Lots of interest in this place. The 1940's are a long ways back. The people here may not like the German in these visitors, but they spend a lot of money here."

"I guess you won't be speaking much German here, will you?" quipped Caroline.

"No, I won't. I will use it only in last resort, and even then..."

Lucas quickly sought to change the subject. "What is our next stop again? Jindrichuv Hradec? Another castle town, I gather. We should leave. Hopefully, we can make it before dark. We don't have a place to stay yet."

With that, the young couple left the restaurant, walked down the narrow street, retrieved their Skoda and took to the winding road leading to the castle town of Jindrichuv Hradec, halfway to Prague.

---

It was 8 o'clock in the evening when Lucas and Caroline arrived in the center of Jindrichuv Hradec and looked for the sign of a hotel.

"Lucas, stop. Here is one. It is the only one I can see."

"OK". Lucas found a parking space on the square, got out and crossed to the entrance of the hotel. On the ground floor was a restaurant, which looked to be more of a bar, with a few patrons milling around. It became obvious very quickly to Lucas that this was not a five star hotel. It looked like it had been there a long time. The office was on the second floor. No one was at the desk, but after Lucas rang the desk bell, a middle-aged woman appeared through a door off the lobby. The lady did not speak English and Lucas was not about to use his German. In any case, the lady managed to indicate that only one room was available - "suite" she managed to say in English. The price was the Czech equivalent of thirty U.S. dollars. Lucas thought, this is not very expensive. I wonder what this is going to look like. Would have preferred two rooms - not sure we're ready for the communal bed yet, but........

The lady took Lucas down the long hall over well-worn carpeting to a room in the back. The place smelled of cigarette smoke and the floor creaked. He could hear activity in at least three of the rooms along the hall, from one of which came boisterous laughter. I'm not sure Caroline is going to go for this, Lucas thought, as he inspected the two-room unit. There was a roll-out bed in the living room that had linoleum flooring. The bedroom had carpeting, although it looked pretty threadbare. The bathroom was miniscule. Definitely Soviet era, he thought.

"OK, madame, we will take it," said Lucas with a nod of his head.

The portly Czech lady nodded back and they proceeded back to the desk where Lucas paid for the night.

"Lucas, this place smells terrible and the floor creaks. I can hear the people in the next room."

"I know, but it's 8:30. We could have continued to roam the streets for another hotel, but it may be the best we can find, given the hour."

After they had put their bags in the room, they descended to the restaurant. The thirty or so patrons turned towards the newcomers and all discussion stopped. New people. Silence. Stares at the pretty girl in shorts and t-shirt. Within seconds, Lucas grabbed Caroline's arm and took her back out the door to the street. "We are not having anything here. Locals only. Smoke is overbearing. Everybody seems to smoke in this country."

Lucas continued as they walked out through the darkened courtyard to the street. "Let's walk around. There have to be better places to have a meal or a drink in this town."

They soon came in front of a large bay window with a restaurant sign above it and through the window, they could see a group of young people at long wooden tables with pitchers of beer. Some people having a good time. It looked much more inviting than what they had just come from. They entered and were received heartily by a young waiter speaking English who quickly found them a table in the corner. 'Band on the Run' with Paul McCartney was playing. They ordered large glasses of local beer (what else?) along with bowls of goulash - and quickly proceeded to relax and smile at their surroundings. There was hope for Jindrichuv Hradec after all.

"Another castle tomorrow. Are you up for it?" asked Lucas after downing half his glass of Pilsner Urquell.

"Might as well. I'm into the history of Bohemia full bore. It's really why I came here. And I could think of worse companions than you to do it with," said Caroline with a teasing look in her eye.

Lucas returned the smile, then added, "Flyer I picked up at the door here says the castle opens at 9:30 AM. First guided tour is at 10. Let's try to make it there for 9:30 and get a place in the tour. The next one is only at 11:30. Leaves us time to get to Tabor in early afternoon. You OK for that?"

"Sure."

"In the meantime," said Lucas, "I will take the couch and you will have the big creaky bed in the bedroom back in the Soviet."

Caroline looked wistfully across the table and responded haltingly, "I was thinking that maybe it's time we got over the friend to friend thing, Lucas."

"Not tonight, Caroline. That room is not very romantic. I think Prague will be more appropriate. It will be better. OK?"

"OK," she replied, looking deeply into Lucas's eyes across the table.

"Caroline, I am into this as well. Let's just get it started right. That smelly hotel is not the place."

They spent the next hour sharing their impressions of the Czech countryside they had passed through and of what they had seen and heard that day. Neither had any idea before this day of the grandeur and splendid beauty of Bohemia.

By the time they left the bistro, it was ten o'clock. Caroline hooked her arm in Lucas's as they walked up the street, past the boisterous crowd seen through the windows of the smoke-filled restaurant of their hotel, up the stairs and down the hall to their room where they took no more than two minutes to drop into deep slumber.

---

"Not the most elaborate of breakfasts, but I will gladly take it," quipped Lucas as he and Caroline buttered their toast, finished off their fruit plates and sipped their coffee. "Sleep OK?"

"Yes, I was fine. Could have slept some more, actually. The shower really woke me up, though."

"I suppose if we would have let the shower run another five minutes, we would have received some warmer water," replied Lucas. "Feel refreshed, though. Ready for some more history today?"

"You bet, as my dad would say."

"Well, it's 8:15 now," said Lucas as he glanced at his watch, "The castle is just a short walk down. Let's try to get over there before it opens and check out the scenery. Another big castle with lots of history. I am getting to appreciate all of this."

"So am I. Really glad I came. Hopefully, I will be able to get to the bottom of where the Webers came from."

Lucas and Caroline finished their coffee and walked out. They managed to secure a spot in the first tour of the castle.

Soon into their tour of the grounds, they were brought to a structure called the Rondel. The sign in front said it was a music pavilion built in 1592 to entertain the nobility with music conducted by musicians located in the basement. The basement? thought Lucas. The guide was explaining in English that the sounds of the music reached the audience on the elaborate marbled ground floor through a hole in the center of it, which Caroline and Lucas could see from where they were standing a few feet away. The musicians were deemed to be of such inferior social standing that they were considered unfit to be in the same room as the nobility assembled for their concerts, which the guide assured everyone were lovely, with the high-ceilinged rotunda providing an ideal acoustical effect.

"Wow," said Caroline. "Go figure. No wonder there was class conflict from time to time over here."

"Amazing," responded Lucas. "Explains a lot why many people left for America."

Lucas grabbed Caroline by the hand; they left the Rondel and got in line for the tour of the main castle. It included a visit of the main living quarters of the families who ruled the castle and the area from the 1300's up to the Second World War. It proved to be another lesson in Bohemian history. "Defenestration. You ever hear that word before?" asked Lucas. The story about Count Slavata had amused him.

"No. Never"

Lucas thought this was a strange and somewhat brutal way to dispose of someone or settle an argument. "Somebody gets thrown out of a window. They call it defenestration. As in French *'par la fenêtre'*. Interesting. She said it was one of many in the history of Bohemia. What a way to deal with discord."

After a quick lunch in the village square, they continued on their way to the town of Tabor. According to the tour book that Caroline had, Tabor was founded in 1420 by a group of Hussites. The Hussites were a sect of Catholicism following the ideas and writings of Jan Hus, who defied the ecclesiastical authorities of the Holy Roman Empire and of the church hierarchy.

Jan Hus was described as the principal predecessor of the Protestant movement that took hold a century later. Caroline read that the town became the seat of the principal and most powerful of the various Hussite sects that emerged in Bohemia, one that was far stricter than the others, inflicting the severest punishments on adultery, perjury and usury. The book's section on Tabor went on to describe the schisms that evolved in the following years between various Taborite factions, one of which was a group of advanced radicals preaching nudism and the communism of women, amongst other things.

"Lucas, I just discovered the origins of free love. A communism of women. Right here in Tabor in the 15th Century."

"Free love in those days? In Europe? The sharing of women in the super-religious times of the 15th Century? Hooo........," wondered Lucas out loud.

"Yep. There was a whole movement that developed here that was essentially communist, opposing all the rites and ornamentations of the Church as well as class distinctions, even the holding of personal property. A Bohemian peasant turned philosopher took it to the extreme, advocating anarchism and voluntary poverty, a society without lords or serfs, Church, property or state, marriage, or laws of any kind. His movement preached, among other things, the application of nudity and free-love - no marriage, everything and everybody were there for the use of everyone, in peace, of course. Didn't last long, though. An opposite faction of Taborites took the anarchists to war and the apostles of peace and freedom were crushed."

"Looks to be a pretty brutal place in the old days," said Lucas. "Isn't Tabor also the name of the place where Christ was taken right after the crucifixion? Mount Tabor or something like that?"

Caroline: "Yes, I do remember that. Yep.... here it is. 'Town named after the place of the Transfiguration of Christ'."

Lucas parked the car in a lot across the bridge at the base of the Old Town. "Time for a beer, and maybe something to eat. Restaurant over there with the big awning looks inviting. Shall we?"

"Sure. I think you are getting to like Czech beer, by the way."

After a beer and a salad, Lucas and Caroline walked the streets of old Tabor, climbed the 200 steps of the Tower, spent a few moments in the Cathedral, basked once again in the vibrant history of Bohemia and made their way back to their little red Skoda and the road to Prague.

They arrived there in early evening and found the hotel in the old city where Caroline had reserved a room. Checking in at the hotel with only one room reserved would have been awkward for the two of them if they had not tacitly acknowledged during the trip they would be sharing a room in Prague. Caroline took Lucas by the hand, opened the door to their room and without turning on a light, lead him to the edge of the bed, where she gently pushed him on to his back, bent over and kissed him on the lips, then slowly let herself down on to the length of his outstretched body.

The two walked hand in hand everywhere over the next four days as they continued their search for Caroline's ancestry and their growing closeness to each other.

---

"I can't believe that eight short weeks ago I was in a prison. Facing a life sentence on the other side of the world. Not certain at all I would get out. Here I am now, free, in Prague, with you and having a wonderful time." Caroline smiled back. Lucas gave her a slight, quick wink of the eye. Their eyes met and lingered for a moment before Lucas continued.

"I shudder to think of what could have happened and what my life could have been. I was terrified. My uncle and grandfather saved my life. The Brandts came to the rescue."

Caroline looked deeply into the eyes of the young man she was falling in love with. "What was going through your mind? In those days and nights in jail?"

"Basically…about life. How fragile it is. How fate, an incident gone wrong can condemn someone. I felt sorry for myself a lot of the time. Not good; not good at all. It was particularly hellish the two days or so before my lawyer uncle Richard got to Singapore. I thought I would crack. He took control though. He told me the plan and gave me hope. Nevertheless, I was scared the whole time I was there, right up until the day it was over."

"I only learned later to what extent my grandfather used his influence to have the charges dropped......." Lucas paused, and then continued. "I will forever be indebted to my uncle and especially to my grandfather. He is getting on. I will try to spend as much time with him as I can. Getting the job in Vienna will bring me closer to him. I'm looking forward to seeing him at his island getaway next week, the family get-away actually, and a pretty nice one at that."

"This is a long way from your question about what was going through my mind. It was terror, Caroline. Terror mixed with more than what I would like to admit of self-pity. I haven't shared these feelings with anyone. I started to with my mother, but didn't get very far. I clammed up about my feelings with my grandfather as well. I was so overjoyed in the two days after being freed that my time with him was taken up with talking about other stuf. About family, getting to know him once more, listening to his stories of his life, of my grandmother who is dead now, of my father, for God's sake, and the many things I did not know about him. But it was real, the anxiety, the fear, the self-pity. I will never wish that on anyone. People who have not spent any length of time in a jail, who have not been confronted with the possibility of a lifetime of incarceration, cannot really understand it. I mean really understand it."

"The release came back in London. It all came out one night. I got really drunk. I will say no more," Lucas said, finishing with a chuckle.

# Chapter 14

On their second day in Prague, Lucas and Caroline drove to Plzen for a meeting at the state archives office for Western Bohemia. Lucas had called there to make an appointment with the assurance that someone who spoke English would be around to answer their questions. The administrator said that all the records for the area in the period of the 1830's to 1860's were in long-hand German. Lucas, fluent in the language, did not see any problem with being able to read the documents they would be presented with the following day.

Caroline was full of enthusiasm as they drove. She was, after all, in love. She had never had nights like the ones they had just had. Lucas was gentle. She had cuddled up in his arms all through each night and was looking forward to doing it again. She was enthralled with him. It appeared to her that Lucas felt the same way....and he did. Caroline was lovely, lively, smart, fun to be with, and very passionate as he had learned over the past day and a half.

They arrived in Plzen. The English-speaking person who was supposed to meet them was not there. Lucas managed to make known his request to inspect the book of births in the period of 1820 to 1840 in the parishes in the immediate vicinity of the village of Ronsperg which had now the Czech name of Pobezovice. The young lady in charge emerged from a back room with four large books and motioned to Lucas and Caroline they could review them in the adjoining reading room.

Caroline had told Lucas that, according to what she learned from the Vienna researcher, Thomas Weber had been born in the Ronsperg area in 1830. She had no information about his wife whose maiden name had been Strauss. After an hour looking through the books, a listing was found of the birth and baptism of a Thomas Weber in the parish of Mutenin in 1828. Lucas could not make out the names of the parents nor the god-parents. Caroline nonetheless was having trouble containing her excitement at the discovery of the birth record of her great-great-grandfather.

The search for the records of a Barbara Strauss, however, proved more elusive. None of the books contained a reference to a Strauss child in the parishes covered. At least not one that Lucas could make out from the difficult Old German script, as he looked for names beginning with an S. Lucas went over the books twice, back to front, but could not find anything about anyone named Strauss. He asked the administrator if there were books of other parishes nearby. Two others were produced, but there was no reference to a Strauss. One of the other researchers in the room who understood and spoke English overhead the discussions and offered to assist in translation with the records administrator. The lady at the counter had observed the frustration of the young couple in the exercise, and through the interpreter who had presented himself, explained that the best way to get through this material was to hire a researcher who was used to dealing in these records and could read what was written. She provided them the name and contact information of an expert researcher who lived not far away and spoke excellent English. An appointment was soon made for 3 PM that afternoon.

After lunch in the city square of Plzen, Lucas and Caroline met with the researcher. Ms. Jagrova told them that many records were held in the offices of larger parishes that had been amalgamated in the 19th Century. Many more old records were held in files confiscated by the Communist government in the 1950's and 60's. If they wanted her to find out who the parents of Thomas Weber were as well as where his wife Barbara Strauss was born and who her parents were, it would take her at least sixty days before she could have the results. She had a lot of work going on. Caroline did not hesitate in confirming the order for the work.

"Well, although it will take some more time, progress is being made", said Caroline enthusiastically.

"I think so. The lady seems to be very good. The records administrator said so. But I can't believe the difficulty of reading the handwriting of the time. Each book, with entries written by different people, was just as difficult to read as the next one, and on and on. And I read German. Just not that German, I guess. Looks like everybody, at least in Bohemia, wrote that way in those days. No typewriters. *Dommage, n'est-ce pas?"*

"*Oui, dommage,* my handsome Anglo-Kraut who speaks a bit of French as well!" responded Caroline playfully.

Lucas and Caroline arrived back in Prague in late afternoon. For their last day in the Czech Republic, they decided to take a boat ride on the river that flowed through Prague and spend the evening in the Old City. Walking back to the Grand Square after the boat ride, they walked past the entrance to the famous old Jewish Cemetery and Museum which Lucas made a note in his mind to visit if he was ever back in Prague. They discovered the popular cook-out stands of sausages, cheeses, pickles, fried dumplings and other Czech favorites, bought a mix of them, got glasses of beer and found a table in the garden behind the stands.

"I love it here, and I think it's rubbing off on my ideas about the guy I'm with, as well."

"It has been nice and I have enjoyed being your bodyguard," said Lucas with a big smile on his face. Grabbing Caroline's hand, he rose and said, "Let's go see what we can find for our friends and families. It would be a shame if we returned empty handed." The two then made their way through the teeming narrow streets of Old Prague inspecting beer mugs, T-

150

shirts, trinkets and candies, then finding their hotel for another night entwined together in amorous embrace.

---

Finishing her breakfast, Caroline said to Lucas, "This has been really something. I come to Vienna to find my roots, you come to find a job, and we end up here, this way. I never would have thought."

"I certainly had no idea, either. I'm not sure I know what we do with this. Kansas City is a long way from London and Vienna."

"Lucas Brandt, I am not going to just let this go and move on to a next stage in my life just like that. I want our thing together to continue. I'm not sure how we are going to do it, but...," she implored.

"I don't want to end it either. The week together has been special. Let's think about how we can do this. This is not going to end."

# Chapter 15

As they passed through Switzerland to Marseille, André was possessed with the thought that his own wife's uncle was the monster who was responsible for the deaths of his grandparents. His whole family on his father's side. Everything gone. Assets that his father could have had, that he could have had. His life would have been different. God damn it! he thought, while vowing to share it with no one. Maybe I will talk about it to Claudia. Maybe I won't. It shakes up everything.

As he drove along, his thoughts drifted to Claudia's connection to the Cobourg-Strauss family. Have to look at the diary again. Who were these people? Could there be something I can work on? What is the connection with Bohemia and the estate there? I will look into it, he thought, as they made their way to the Cote d'Azur and home.

André hired a researcher in Vienna to look into all he could on the Cobourg-Strauss family. He received the report three weeks later. The family had been and still was prominent in Vienna. There was a Cobourg-Strauss who was a justice on the highest court of Austria and another who was owner of a large media company. The Karl Cobourg-Strauss who was Claudia's father's good friend from university according to the entry in her mother's dairy, was mentioned as one of the wealthiest men in Austria before his death in 1996.

For over 300 years the family owned an estate in Western Bohemia around the town of Ronsperg. Silver and quartz mines were the source of the family's wealth. The Ronsperg estate had been in the hands of the von Trauttdorf family from the early 1620's to later that century when the principal heir of the family, Catherine von Trauttdorf, married a Wilhelm Cobourg-Strauss, and inherited the estate and the castle. The estate was owned by the Cobourg-Strauss family until 1948 when it was confiscated by the Communists.

Among other details, the report contained a reference to an incident at the Ronsperg castle in 1862. A member of the family was thrown out of a window. Somebody else getting thrown out a window, thought André. This seemed to be a popular method of disposal with these people. A newspaper report of an interview with Karl Cobourg-Strauss, the scion of the family in the 1960's who had become an influential crusader against Anti-Semitism, related his disgust with various aspects of his family's background in dealing with Jews. The report divulged that one of the Cobourg-Strauss brothers of the early 1860's was thrown out of window of the castle tower for having sold large quantities of silver to Jewish precious metals traders in Prague, which was against the edicts of the Austrian emperor and was destabilizing the currency. This apparently caused great distress to the patriarch of the family who was close to the regime in Vienna. It was rumored as well that the silver had been re-sold to the government of Prussia, Austria's arch-enemy. The brother who was murdered was a favorite of the family and the incident caused a family schism. A sister and her husband who ran the estate as well as the mines on the land left and went to Vienna. Another brother left as well. With the loss of the estate manager who had been brilliant in building the mining business of the family, the estate lost a considerable amount of its value over the ensuing decade and beyond. It regained its solid economic foundation only years later through the effective management of a grandson of the patriarch. In the section of the report dealing with the extended Cobourg-Strauss ancestry, André discovered that the family descended from the Hradec - Slawak dynasty of Southern Bohemia.

Well, well. His own wife was a descendant of that man as well! This is all very interesting, thought André as he put down the report and went to bed. I have more than one reason to do something about old Erik. Those Bendt bastards! A Jew killer and a cheap old son-of-a bitch! Claudia.. Claudia....what do I do about Claudia and her ancestry in all of this? She comes from a wealthy family. Marco is on to me. Close to two million now. I have to do something. Can some retribution come out of all of this?

An hour later, not able to sleep, André sat up in bed and thought he had an answer.

He worked out the details in his mind.

Three hours later, he bolted up in bed. The dream was back. This time, the face of the separator in front of the line of boxcars was the one of Erik Brandt.

# Chapter 16

Lucas had been looking forward to seeing his grandfather as well as spending a few days on the island.

Erik's cherished property was a large villa near the center of the castle village of Giglio Castello on Isola del Giglio island, nine miles off the coast of Tuscany in the Tyrrhenian Sea.

The wood-paneled study with a fireplace at the end overlooked one of the three squares of the village three stories below. From the big double window that opened to the outside, Lucas could observe the cafe across the square and the shoe repair shop next to it. It had exactly the same facade as when he was a boy. The elderly cobbler would always greet him with a hearty welcome and repair his sandals and the fine leather boots that his grandfather would seem to wear everywhere and insist on keeping in excellent, polished condition. He remembered the shop with its fine leather and shoe polish aromas filling the air with a pungent, pleasant odor. Earlier that morning, Lucas had gone down to the square, crossed the little plaza to the shop where Giuseppe immediately recognized him and gave him a huge bear hug of a greeting. "You are back. Look at you! You are no longer that ten-year old scamp I once knew." With a mischievous look in his eyes, the old man looked Lucas up and down. "You look prosperous. Where have you been? I am so glad to see you." Lucas spent the next half-hour filling the old man in on where his life had taken him since the days of his childhood on the island. He left out any reference to Singapore, however, and when the arrival of a customer interrupted their exchange, they agreed to have a glass of wine at the cafe next door before the day was out.

Lucas understood the magic of the place for his grandfather. Erik's own father had inherited it from his mother's family who had acquired it sometime in the 1880's. It was precious. Lucas was glad it was in the family and had no doubt that it would remain so. The thought of that reminded him to ask his grandfather what had transpired at the family meeting after the death of his grandmother the year before. He had received little information from that. His father had not been forthcoming on what had transpired and he and Erik had not discussed the matter in Singapore. In fact, his father had not spoken to him at all since the death of his grandmother. Lucas was in India when she died and by the time he learned of her death, there was not enough time for him to make it to the funeral service.

Lucas had arrived at the villa late the previous day and had not had the chance to speak at any length with his grandfather. As they prepared their dinner together that evening, Lucas observed that Erik appeared a bit on edge.

"So, what's the job situation for you? How does it look?" asked Erik as he sliced some tomatoes and Lucas uncorked a bottle of vintage Chianti from the wine cellar.

"Pretty good, Dada. May end up working for UNIDO out of Vienna. You must surely know of UNIDO from your diplomatic service days, I would think?"

"Oh, yes. Had lots of dealings with the U.N. agencies as I travelled around. Ran into their officials quite often at receptions when in the developing world." After a brief pause, he continued, "The Singapore affair with them? What did they say? They must have learned of it. World Bank and UNIDO and the other U.N. agencies are pretty tight."

"They knew about it. My Bank boss told them all about it and made the recommendation anyway. I am grateful to him. Without his endorsement, it would indeed be very difficult to get another job in the development business." Lucas continued as he poured the wine. "The guys I saw in Vienna were very upfront about the issue and said it would not prevent them from hiring me. The recommendation from Washington was top-notch from someone they obviously knew and trusted. Only problem may be a question of budget. In any case, it is August and nothing gets approved in August. I will most likely hear from them when I am back in London. I hope it works, as I don't have a backup plan. Not yet, anyway."

"By the way, my time with Mother has been great. It has been good for her and it has been good for me as well. Reconnected with my cousins Ivan and Vincent. Helped Uncle David in the meantime. Not something I would want to do for a living, I might add, but David is great, a big *bon vivant*, a generous soul. I like him a lot. It has been fun."

"Good. I have always liked your mother. She was the best thing that ever happened to Georg, but he messed it up. I was not happy with the break-up. Apart from my disappointment with my son, the break-up took my grandson and granddaughter away from me. No more fishing with you. No more bocce on the square, no more gelato in the village." After a pause, Erik continued, "But now you are here. You said last night you were in Prague. Tell me about it. Why did you go there?" Erik asked. Lucas noticed a brief frown on his grandfather's face as he asked the question about the trip to Prague.

Lucas related his encounter with Caroline in Vienna, the time they spent together there, her invitation to go with her to Prague, the visits of the castle towns on the way, the side trip to Plzen and Caroline's search for her European roots. Erik listened intently, but made no comment as he finished the preparation of the meal of pasta and salad.

After an hour and the finishing of the Chianti and talk about football - Erik was a lifelong fan of Bayern Munich and Lucas of Arsenal from his youth in London - Erik put his glass down, paused a moment, then looked Lucas directly in the eye across the table.

"There is something I must tell you, Lucas. Actually, there are two things I must tell you. I have refrained from sharing them with anyone, even with my own sons. You are here. Although I feel well, have no real ailments, I may die tomorrow and not have the chance to explain these things to anyone. Who knows. But you are here and I cannot hold it any longer. What I am going to tell you will, I hope, allow you to make sense of what we spoke about that last evening in Singapore, make sense of the strange family life we have had as well as allow me to get some weight off my shoulders." The elderly gentleman with the always elegant, distinguished demeanor paused for a moment, then continued, "I am getting old. Secrets can eat at you and they are very much eating at me these days - more than ever. For far too long, I might add. You will most certainly understand why."

Across the table, Lucas was wondering what this could possibly be about. He quickly understood why his grandfather had been on edge.

"I told you about my brother and my change of name to Brandt before the war. There is more to it. I said my real name was Braun. It wasn't. It was Bendt. My brother's name was Helmut Bendt. He was my twin." The words kept flowing. "And he became a monster. After the war, I learned he had been the head of the Gestapo in Prague, responsible for the deaths of thousands of people. I have always been terrified of this coming

160

to the light of day, that my real name would be exposed, that the link to my brother would be made known. That through this, the whole line of my family would be forever tarnished. As a consequence, I have been obliged to deny, suppress entirely if you will, the family name from my past, in essence become someone else. My quest to live up to the family heritage, to the legacy of my father and the distinguished family line before him, was a powerful force, particularly after I learned of the deeds of my brother. It affected my marriage. Tore it apart, actually. Isabel knew all of this, of course, and forever berated me about my obsession with it, although she kept it to herself, as far as I can tell. She never shared the truth of this with anyone else. I am pretty certain of that. But it ruined our marriage, a marriage that had started so well. We loved each other."

"Why am I telling you this, Lucas? It is because someone has to know. I will die some day. The link between my brother and I could become known. Many, many people who suffered from the Holocaust are still alive as are their descendants. If no one in our family knows the truth and I am not around to talk about it, to confirm, correct or deny, whatever comes out will be what people retain, understand, believe."

The old man paused, rose and fetched a glass of water, then sat down once again and continued, "You have just arrived from Prague. I would never be able to go there, and I never have. Thankfully, it was behind the Iron Curtain during my working years. I never went. Thank God, as you must understand. My own brother was called The Butcher of Prague."

The retired diplomat paused, reached for a tissue, dabbed his eyes, then continued. "That brings me to the second thing I want to tell you of. It has a connection to Bohemia, if not to Prague. It has a lot to do with my estrangement from your grandmother. It wasn't only about my obsession with the family legacy, although the two are connected."

Lucas had been listening intently. He had not said a word as his grandfather opened up. He could tell there was more to come.

"Your aunt Claudia is not my daughter. I am not her real father. It is difficult for me to tell you this, as it will surely tarnish your view of your grandmother. It should not. I drove her to it. Your father and your uncles Richard and Karl do not know this. Claudia does not either. At least I don't think she does. Isabel promised me she would never tell the children. I explain."

For a moment, Lucas was stunned. But then, he realized he was not all that surprised.

Erik went on with the story of Claudia's birth.

Lucas was silent, captivated by the unfolding story of his family.

"So, Lucas, why am I telling you this, along with the truth of my name and my brother? One, it has a lot to do with the dysfunctions of the family that you have observed. We started this discussion in Singapore, but I stopped. I only went so far.

162

After my returning here, I decided I would find a good time to complete the story. Two, although I am not sure of it, I believe Claudia's husband is up to something. Someone in the family needs to know this, and I'm afraid it can't be your father or your uncles, for reasons I will explain."

Lucas continued to sit there, listening to his grandfather.

"I have to first of all tell you what I told your father, Richard, Karl and Claudia last year after your grandmother's funeral, about what I intended to do with the family properties." Erik explained the plan. "Claudia had not expressed any fundamental objection to it. That changed. Her visits here have all had the same intent - a request that I change the will to cede her the property. She said it would only be fair. The boys had their own homes and other possessions and were doing well. They could take the proceeds for the sale of the other properties and do what they wished with the money. She would forego her share of those in exchange for getting the villa here. The urgency of this all has to do with her husband's affairs. He's in trouble. Everybody in business in Marseille knows it. It is clear he wants to get at the family assets to solve his problems and is using Claudia. I am not going to oblige."

Erik paused, then went on. "Her second visit, sometime in April, happened after she called me and said she was coming to the island. We had to talk, she said. I told her if it was going to go in the same direction it did the first time around, she should stay in Marseille. She said she was coming anyway and hung up.

Three days later, she was at the door with her husband. Although starting off pleasantly enough, the visit ended up going the same way as the one a couple months before. I had to ask them to leave. While they were here, however, her husband had taken what I thought to be an inordinate degree of attention to the interior of the place. Granted, he had never been here before, but just the same…I did not have a good feeling and don't to this day. I don't like him. I never have."

"After that incident, I decided that this property was too precious to dispose of. It would remain in the family for everyone to use, with such to be worked out, and changed my will accordingly. My lawyer in Bonn, by the way, has a copy of it. The property is a jewel. It has been in the family for over a hundred years. I decided it would stay that way. Sometime in June, after the trip to Singapore, Claudia showed up again, unannounced and unaccompanied. I said no. I told her about my decision that the property would stay in the family for everyone to use. I would leave sufficient funds for its upkeep and taxes for twenty years after my death. She erupted as only she can do. She insisted I sell off the other properties, market or no market. Sell them now. She wanted her share. I told her I was not going to do that. I was not going to upset the optimal disposition of our high value family property merely to solve her husband's financial difficulties. It was up to him to get himself out of whatever trouble he was in. Well, she was not happy. It ended badly. She slammed the door and went off."

"Why am I telling YOU this, Lucas, and not your father or your uncles?" placing the emphasis on the YOU in what he was saying. "It is because I could not and cannot still, bear to tell them of the infidelity of their mother. I cannot bear the thought of telling them their sister is only their half-sister. Letting them know their staunchly Catholic mother would let herself be seduced by a man fifteen years younger than she is too much for me to assume. I was the cause of it and yet I don't want it to ruin the last years of my life with my boys. Can you understand that?"

"Yes, I can, grandfather. I respect you and I understand. You must know that."

"Thank you, Lucas."

With a sigh, what seemed to Lucas to be one of relief, Erik looked across the table and made a final request "Lucas, you must know I am asking you to keep this to yourself, and only yourself. Can I ask you to do that?"

"Yes, Dada, you can. I am actually grateful you are telling me all this. I now understand many things and ..I don't blame you…and I am grateful this place will stay in the family." Lucas got up, went around the table, and put his arms around the shoulders of his elderly grandfather from behind. He tightly hugged the proud, aristocratic German gentleman with tears in his eyes who had just unloaded the two essential secrets of his life and could say no more.

Lucas spent the following day with his grandfather fishing in the bay off the west coast of the island and in the afternoon playing bocce and having a dish of gelato in the village, just as they often did years before. Erik drove Lucas down the hill to the ferry dock the next morning and the young man made his way to Rome and his flight to London.

# Chapter 17

Lucas had been back in London for a few days when he received the letter from Vienna. UNIDO was offering him the job they had discussed - Development Economist for the Middle East and Africa, starting November 1. Later that evening, he placed a call to Caroline. This was Lucas' second telephone call with Caroline since his return to London. He had phoned her two days before to see how her return had went and to talk briefly about his stay with his grandfather. Caroline recognized the U.K. number displayed on the handset and eagerly jabbed the talk button with an exuberant "Hi there! Good to hear your voice again!" quickly following.

"I got the job. Received the letter today. Start November 1. Am very happy about it. And, like I intimated Monday, I want to go see you before I start," said a buoyant Lucas Brandt into the phone. He explained that he would be going to Vienna for an orientation session for new employees the third week of

September but that October was open for him to do whatever he wanted with his time.

"Wow! Yes! When can you come? I'm ready and willing! Yes!" she shouted back.

"I'm serious. I want to see you and I could do it in October. I have to go to DC anyway to clear up a couple of things from my time there before I start work. I could fly to Kansas City from DC, stay over a few days, then return to London from there. What do you say?"

"Great. Yes! It will be so good to see you. Wait a minute..... we could maybe make a real long weekend of it. I have to go back home soon and pick up stuff for my place here. I was going to do it anyway and had the OK from my boss - a long weekend over which to do it. Just have to tell him which weekend it will be. You could come here to Kansas City and the next day we could go to Westmoreland and spend a day or so there - it's two and a half hours by car from here. You can meet my parents if you are up for that and get a feel for what the real Kansas is all about." Caroline paused a moment, then continued, "You will have a separate bedroom, though," chuckled Caroline over the phone. "We will have to do what we want to do in Kansas City."

"All right," responded Lucas while Caroline continued, "we could go back to Kansas City on the Monday and you could decide when to return to London from there. Maybe stay a few days with me in KC?"

"OK. Sounds good. I'm not too sure about the parents, though. I will leave that in your hands. You sure you want to do that - have me at your parents' house?" asked Lucas, somewhat mischievously.

"Yes, I do, Lucas. It will be fine. They already know about you. I told them all about our trip. Didn't take long for my mom to figure out that we slept together. Don't worry about it, Lucas. My Dad and Mom may be farmers but they are not prudes. I went to big liberal KU, after all. They know what that is all about, so they have gotten used to the fact their little girl is no longer a little girl." After a short pause, Caroline blurted into the phone "I will be so happy to seeee youuu!"

"Me too. Let me get on to flights and stuff and then get back to you. Second weekend of October? Could we do it then?"

"Four weeks from now. Yes! We could do it then......Love you," replied Caroline.

"Right on. Love you too. Will e-mail you what I can arrange for DC and Kansas City. Speak soon. Bye. Take care."

Caroline put down the phone and had a wonderful feeling that she would soon be seeing her newfound love once again. The future will be the future from here on in.

---

After hanging up, Lucas placed a call to his grandfather on the island. "Dada, I got the job in Vienna. Start November 1. Just wanted to let you know. How are you doing, by the way?"

"I am fine, Lucas, and congratulations on the job. Your stay with me last week was very enjoyable, young man. I truly enjoyed it. I realized how much I missed you, all those years. And, I plan to go see you in Vienna. I can't stay here all the time, in any case. Can get lonely, although I guess I manage. Giuseppe looks after me. At least he says he does and there is my housekeeper, who is very loyal. She was not around during your stay - she was at her daughter's on the mainland that week," replied Erik. After a pause, he continued "Anna's daughter, Sylvia - you remember Anna, Lucas? - will be here for a few days next week on holiday with her husband. I look forward to it. Glad to have visitors. Great place for it, and you know you are welcome any time."

"Very good, Dada," replied Lucas, "you will hear from me regularly. All the best," and hung up.

# Chapter 18

## Marseille, September 1999

"Marco, I need to talk to you. Can we meet in the next couple of days?" André asked over the telephone.

"What about? Before anything else, you are going to tell me how you are going to pay me. André? Do you get it? I have been a good boy, a good cousin to you, but time is running out. I need you to take care of this, once and for all. You better have a good word for me."

"Well, that is exactly what I want to talk to you about. So, when can we meet? I suggest we meet halfway."

"No, André, you come here. Antonia is not around anymore. We'll talk right here. I will have a lunch waiting for you. Tuesday at 12:30. Just be here. See you then." Click

André put down the phone and wondered if his cousin would buy into his plan.

**Vienna...**

The two-day orientation session was finishing up and Lucas was looking forward to the weekend. He had booked his return flight with a stopover in Prague. He had noticed in the Daily Telegraph sports section that Plzen's FC Viktoria football club would be playing Juventus of Turin in an exhibition match in Plzen on Saturday. He decided to take the chance of finding a ticket on site. While in Plzen, he could take a tour of the famous Pilsner Urquell Brewery in the morning, something he was unable to do the month before with Caroline. He would spend Sunday in Prague before continuing on to London the following day.

As he was entering the industrial eastern edge of Plzen, something written on the side of what appeared to be an abandoned warehouse off to the right caught his eye. In fading black letters on the top section of the old brick building was written what appeared to be GRALLA METALLARBEITEN - Gralla Metalworks.

Lucas slowed down and looked more closely at the building and the barely legible German lettering on its side. Gralla...that was his Aunt Claudia's husband's name. Huh....could there be a connection? But the man is French, thought Lucas as he pondered the thought of a possible connection of his aunt's maligned husband to whatever existed here in Plzen.

In any case, whatever enterprise here that went by the name of Gralla and that advertised itself in German, existed here either before or during the war; certainly not afterward. No signs in German were put up anywhere here after 1945. Lucas continued on his way into the city, soon recognizing the tell-tale green and gold logo of Pilsner Urquell on a huge smokestack. There was a sign for tours at the archway of the entrance to the complex. He drove through the archway, encountered an employee at the edge of the parking area and learned that the next tour would begin a few minutes from then at 10AM. Great...gives me ample time to get to the stadium by 3 - he could clearly see the light standards of the football stadium rising above the outlying buildings of the brewery complex.

Three hours later it took no more than five minutes for Lucas to find a scalper with a ticket. Double the regular price. Lucas hesitated for only a moment. Either this or no game in Plzen, thought Lucas, as he paid the man. It was a good fast-paced game before a packed house in boisterous support of their team, but Juventus was a powerhouse, more polished than the Viktoria side and the game finished in a 4-2 victory for the Italian club. After the game, Lucas found a restaurant a few blocks away in the old part of the town, had a plate of goulash and a beer, collected his rented car and made his way back to Prague. His thoughts turned to the Gralla sign on the building. Have to look up the name of Gralla Metallarbeiten when I get back to London. There is a Gralla in our family, after all, thought Lucas, as he recalled what his grandfather had related to him about Claudia, the surprising story of her true parentage and the troubles he had with she and her husband.

The next morning Lucas walked the few blocks from his hotel off Charles Street to the Jewish Cemetery and Museum. After touring the cemetery, he entered the museum. He quietly walked around the stark bare rooms of the cavernous little building with all the names on the walls. On his way out, he passed the glassed-in exhibits of sketches and photographs of children and in the last one observed photographs of German officers gathered in front of trains of people. His eyes quickly came upon the face of a figure that he thought he recognized, but could not place it. At that moment and before he had the chance to read the inscription below the grainy photo, a tour guide arrived with a clutch of tourists and Lucas was encouraged to move toward the door. The thought of the man in the photo left his mind.

# Chapter 19

**London, September 1999**

The search in the British Library for information on Gralla Mettalarbeiten did not take long. He found on microfiche a German-language directory of European manufacturers published in 1935. The entry for Gralla Mettalarbeiten of Czechoslovakia stated that the company made kitchen utensils, had plants in Pilsen (called Plzen now) and Bratislava as well as Krakow in Poland. The company was owned by the Gralla family, led by a Maurice Gralla. With the help of the librarian, Lucas found further information on the enterprise from a 1947 Vienna newspaper article on what had happened to the most significant Czech business enterprises that had existed prior to the war. It said Gralla Mettalarbeiten was one of the many Jewish-owned enterprises that had been taken over by the Nazis and converted to war production. The article went on to say that, like most other Czech facilities converted to war production, the former

Gralla-owned factories had been destroyed by Allied bombing raids in 1944 and 1945 and no longer existed. No mention was made of what had happened to the pre-war owners.

Maurice Gralla. Jewish. André related to him somehow? Pursue it further? Could there be a connection?

The Paris office of the Simon Wiesenthal Center was helpful. Lucas had remembered that the Wiesenthal organization was the premier source of information on the Holocaust, on its victims and its perpetrators. Its European office was in Paris. Lucas explained on the phone what he was looking for and asked if it would be possible to review any pertinent materiel the center would have on the Jewish Gralla family that lived in Pilsen Czechoslovakia before the war. Lucas' respondent on the line suggested that such was quite likely and that Lucas should come to the office in Paris. The center did not provide the sort of information he was looking for other than in person. The lady suggested, however, he could perhaps contact The Holocaust Center of the U.K. in London. She said that the Center there could very well have the information he is looking for and if not, work with the Paris Wiesenthal office to obtain it for him. He would have to present his bona fides to the Center and they could go from there. Lucas proceeded to call the number in London. It was arranged for him to meet the archives section head the following morning.

Within hours, Lucas learned that Maurice Gralla and many family members including his wife, Hanna Gralla, born Hanna

Gersten, of Pilsen, had been rounded up by the Gestapo in late 1941, transported to the collection center at Terezin, and eventually perished at Auschwitz. The information stated that the names of the Grallas were among the 77,000 Czech Jews listed on the walls of the Jewish Museum of Prague. It stated that apparently all family members had been shipped from Pilsen to Terezin in 1941, with the exception of a son Joseph who had left Czechoslovakia for France in the 1930's. It was the only information the center had on other members of the family. As part of his request for information, Lucas, remembering the revelations of his grandfather about his own brother three weeks before, asked the Center if they had any information on a Helmut Bendt, who had apparently been in the Gestapo during the war.

The results came back with the confirmation that a Helmut Bendt was the head of the Gestapo for Prague and western Czechoslovakia from 1941 until 1944. My God, the man in the photo at the Museum. That was him! Dada's brother! The Butcher of Prague. No wonder grandfather never wanted to go there. Lucas immediately understood that his grandfather's brother would have been responsible for the deportation and ultimate deaths of the people who could very well have been the entire family or close to it, of his grandfather's son-in-law! Could it be true? Lord God, exclaimed Lucas under his breath.

Does Dada know this? Does Claudia's husband know this? Who was Joseph Gralla? Is he still alive? Did he have a family? Lucas recognized that what he was in the process of discovering was explosive. Who in the family knew all of it or even parts of it? Is André part of that Gralla family?

Lucas found the telephone number of the office of public records of France in Paris and called. In his broken French, he asked how he could obtain information on a Joseph Gralla, who had lived in France starting sometime in the 1930's. Lucas was directed to the bureau of vital statistics where he could make a request by sending a fax with the name of the individual, place of birth and any other information that would identify the individual. The office would send the results by mail to a return address. The person requesting the information would receive, along with the results of the search, an invoice for 20 Euros. Lucas faxed the request for marriage, death, birth records of children of a Joseph Gralla, place of birth, Pilsen/Plzen Czechoslovakia.

A week later, Lucas received the marriage record of a Joseph Gralla and a Francesca Scalia in Marseille in 1954, the 1979 death record of a Joseph Gralla born 1920 in Czechoslovakia, and a copy of the birth record of a boy André Gralla, born in 1955 to a Joseph and Francesca Gralla. Wow! It's all there, he thought. André's whole family, with the exception of his father, was exterminated by the Nazis, and his father-in-law's own brother was in charge of the operation.

"Oouf", he sighed. Grandfather knows what he was doing, what he was responsible for. All of it. But......André...... does he know all this?

# Chapter 20

## Kansas, October 1999

Caroline was on the phone with the county records office about the results of her research in Austria and Bohemia.

"Bonnie, I just wanted to let you know that I am back from Vienna and a whole series of places in the Czech Republic. I learned a lot, and more is coming."

"Very good, Caroline. I was wondering how you got along over there."

"I've got a much better idea of who Thomas Weber was, but it's not over. There are still a lot of gaps. I just wanted to let you know and thank you once again for helping me get started."

"Well, I think you should try to get into the rectory of the old St. Joseph's church. I told you there were a lot of community and personal records going back a long ways somewhere in that old building. The Bohemians were a close knit group and did everything through their church. You oughta talk to the priest in Wamego and see if you can't get in there. He looks after it -

supposedly, anyway. You may find some stuff that adds to what you've found. I would bet on it."

"I'm going to do just that. I'm home on the weekend and will pay a visit to Father Kurtz at St. Bernard's. Once again, thank you much, Bonnie. Take care."

Father Frank Kurtz, answered the knock on the door. The tall middle-aged priest noticed through the window that the caller was the young daughter of Raymond Weber who had a big farm north of town on Adams Creek Road. He had not seen her in a long time. What was her name? Caroline. Yes, Caroline. He had heard she had gone to KU.

"Well, well, Caroline Weber, what a pleasant surprise. Haven't seen you in a dog's age. What brings you here, my dear?" asked the congenial priest who everybody called Father Frank. He loved to play the role of the kindly priest looking after his flock, but managed to do it without pretense or overbearance.

"Can I come in, Father? I have something to ask of you."

"Come in and sit down. Can I get you something? There is a fresh pot of coffee in the kitchen," asked the priest, while gesturing Caroline to the table in the dining room.

"No, no. Thank you just the same. Yes, Father, it has been some time since I have been around. You probably know I was at KU. Graduated in June and just started a job in Kansas City."

"Well, very good. Congratulations. What can I do for you?" asked the priest.

"Well, a few months ago, I started some research on my dad's ancestors. Went to Austria and the Czech Republic this summer as a matter of fact. Learned a lot, but a lot still remains to be found. Apparently, there is a lot of information on the old Bohemian community of Flush in the rectory of the old church there. There may be stuff there that would allow me to piece together the puzzle of my great-great-grandfather and what he did or did not do."

"I see. You may be right. There is a lot of material in drawers over there, I'm afraid. I never went through it," replied the priest.

"He was controversial, I have been told. He bought a lot of land in the state and then disposed of it. Died poor. Very strange. My own father and grandfather have never wanted to dig into any of it, but I do. Bonnie Williams at the records office in Westmoreland has helped. She told me there could be information in the files at the rectory about the Webers and suggested I contact you."

Father Frank replied, "I will try to help you, but there are some things about that church and the parish there that you should know. I have been here for twenty years and over that time, I have learned a lot about the history of the place. There is a lot of stuff there. I would like to accompany you. As a matter of fact, I think I will have to. The old man who has the keys to the rectory will most probably only let you have them if I am with you. He's a nasty old codger. You go there alone and it may not work out too well.

The priest leaned forward as he continued, "The long-time parish priest, Father Biehler, apparently never mentioned the records to anyone. I'm told he never looked into them - didn't care, I guess. So, there are files there, but I have no idea what they contain. What I do know is that years ago, I believe in the 1920's or 30's, some parishioners and the parish priest at the time learned or at least believed that the church had been built in the 1890's with stolen money and that the records of this were in files housed in the rectory. Something about all this being in a newspaper article years before. The caretaker of the time was apparently hired to destroy all the files. That was what the parishioners and the priest were led to believe. Turns out he didn't do anything to those files at all - just said he did. Just before he died in the late 40's, he charged his son to continue the caretaking duties. That man is the man who we are going to go see to get the keys. Clarence Seitz is a bit dim-witted. He is also somewhat dangerous, as I said earlier. Anybody who approaches his old house on the road just outside Wabaunsee is met with a shotgun blast fired into the air. Nobody goes there. He travels three or four times a year to the rectory in Flush, goes inside, looks around, comes out and goes back to his place. We tolerate it. He's getting old; probably in his late seventies now and won't live forever. In the meantime, he takes his role of caretaker very seriously. His dad told him to. It's a bit sad. Hopefully, we will be

182

able to see what's in the files without too much trouble from Clarence. Maybe there is something there about your ancestors. We'll see."

Father Kurtz spread his hands and rose up from his chair, "It's Saturday today. I have a baptism later this afternoon. We can go to Wabaunsee tomorrow, Caroline. At least I think so, unless the ladies' auxiliary has something planned for tomorrow which they haven't told me about. We will go after lunch. Meet me here at 1 o'clock. We'll take my car. Clarence knows it. All right?"

"Yes, Father. I will be here. See you tomorrow."

---

Caroline arrived back at the farm and as she came through the door, her mother announced that she had received a call from Bonnie Williams.

Caroline placed the call. "Bonnie, how are you? Just as well that you called. I saw the priest in Wamego today. What's up?"

"I remembered something else I wanted to tell you. Two weeks ago, I was at my cousin Linda's place and the subject of the church in Flush came up. Seems somebody wants to build a feed storage place across the road, next to the cemetery. We were talking about the need to consult the archdiocese in Kansas City about the land. The church still owns it. Linda is a town councilor, you know. The subject of the rectory and the St. Joe's parish information that's in there came up. Linda said her great uncle Charlie, now 92, apparently knew a lot about that. Caroline, I think it's worth it to give ol' Charlie Schreiber a call. I have his number here. I told Linda about your interest and she suggested it."

"Great. What's the number?" replied Caroline as she looked for a pen. "I will call him. It could be timely. Father Kurtz is accompanying me tomorrow to try to get access to the rectory. Whatever else is known about the history of the community will be appreciated. I'll let you know what happens. All the best."

Caroline then placed the call.

After six or seven rings, a woman answered. "Schreiber place."

"Hello, I am looking for Mr. Charles Schreiber. Could he be there?" asked Caroline.

"Who's speakin', dear?" asked the woman in a raspy voice.

"This is Caroline Weber, daughter of Raymond Weber on Adams Creek Road. I would like to speak with Mr. Schreiber."

"Well, he's not here right now, dearie. Went up to Fostoria for the weekend to see his grandson. He'll probably be back tomorrow. I suggest you try to call back end of day tomorrow. Could you do that, hun?"

"Thank you, ma'am. I will try tomorrow. You have a nice evening."

The next day, Caroline went to the 11 o'clock Mass with her parents, taking her own car. The Webers were long time parishioners of St. Bernard's and Lorraine was well known in the community, having been in charge of most of the cultural activities in the town for years - the historical society, the drama

184

club and the annual art exhibit, amongst others. It was how she occupied her time. After Mass, Father Kurtz hurried outside to catch Caroline on the front steps, as she and her parents were exchanging greetings with parishioners. "Caroline, I can't go with you today, after all. As I suspected, the ladies have me going to their social at 2. Got word of that before Mass. Then I have my weekly visit to the old folks home across town at 4. We can go down to Wabaunsee next weekend, though, if you are around. Really sorry about this, Caroline."

"Understand. It was pretty short notice. Not sure I will be back next weekend, though. I do know that I will be back two weeks from now," Caroline replied, thinking about the visit from Lucas for the long weekend. "I'll let you know. But, Father, where exactly does the man live?"

"His place, if I remember correctly, is the third one on the right just after the bridge over the creek at the far edge of town. In any case, it is the place where there is an old beat-up red mailbox at the end of the road with an ancient rusting tractor sittin' in the field. Must still be there. Been there for ages. But, my dear, you should not go there alone. Don't do it. Better if we wait until you are back. I should be with you."

"You're probably right, Father Frank. I'll take your advice," replied Caroline.

She found her parents who were chatting with some other people on the sidewalk in front of the church and told them she would meet them back at the farm.

The hell with it, she thought as she got behind the wheel. I'm going to see if I can't talk to the old man. Can't wait forever to get into that old rectory. He'll see I'm a woman, not some guy in a pick-up truck who could be trouble. Mr. Seitz, here I come.

It didn't take long for Caroline to drive through the hamlet a few miles from Wamego. Only a few houses remained with the highway the only paved street, with dirt lanes leading off to the left and right of the main thoroughfare. A run-down old store with a Pabst Blue Ribbon neon sign in the window was the only commercial establishment she could see. She drove slowly towards the creek and saw further on the red mailbox at the end of the road.

Sure enough, there's the old tractor, thought Caroline, as she turned into the road. She had to be careful. The road was not in good shape, with many potholes. As the slow-moving Civic approached the yard in front of the house with a decaying tilted front porch inhabited by an old couch that seemed to be missing a leg or two, the loud *Crack!* of a gunshot rang out, splitting the quiet of the Sunday afternoon. Birds flew up from beside the barn. Caroline could not see where the gunshot came from. But she could hear the load voice of someone using a bull-horn.

"Whoever you are, you get the hell out-a-here, you hear!"

Caroline stopped the car, gingerly opened the car door, trying to locate the source of the voice, "Mr. Seitz, my name is Caroline Weber from Westmoreland. Don't mean to bother you, but can I speak with you? I have something to ask of you."

186

"No, you can't. Now, like I said, you get the hell out of here or I will put some buckshot into that fancy car of yours. This is private property and you are trespassing, woman. Now leave!"

"Please, Mr. Seitz. I don't mean any harm," yelled Caroline towards the voice coming from somewhere in the house twenty yards away. "Father Kurtz from Wamego was to come with me but he couldn't. It's about the old St. Joe's Church in Flush. Please."

Crack! The loud retort of the shotgun rang out. "Now, I told you to leave. You hear? That old church in Flush is my business and nobody else's. Next time, this gun's gonna put buckshot into the side of your car. Understand? Now get the hell down that road and outta here!"

"All right. I'm sorry I bothered you. Goodbye, Mr. Seitz." Caroline got back into the car, turned around in the yard and drove down the road. Father Frank was right. I should have waited to have him come with me.

A bearded old man in blue coveralls with a toothpick in the corner of his mouth and a sawed-off shotgun in his hand emerged from behind the corner of the house and wondered why someone would want to know something about that old church. "Humph. First time anybody has tried to find anything about that place in twenty years. My daddy's old church. Have to protect it. He told me to."

Later that Sunday afternoon Caroline placed another call to Charlie Schreiber.

"Hello, this is Charlie."

"Mr. Schreiber, this is Caroline Weber from Westmoreland. I hope I'm not bothering you. I'd like to talk to you about something if you don't mind."

"Weber. You must be related to Raymond Weber over on Adams Creek Road. No other Webers around here anymore." replied the old man.

"Yes, I am his daughter. Bonnie Williams and her cousin Linda, who I believe you are also related to, suggested I call you about some of the affairs of my grandfather, Andrew Weber. I gather you were friends with him. Would that be possible, sir?"

"Why, young lady, I would be happy to. Yes, your granddaddy was indeed a good friend of mine. He died far too young, by the way. Must be close to thirty years now. I would be glad to talk to you about whatever you want to know. Why don't you come over now? You must be only ten minutes away. I'm on Wheaton Road just before the junction with the highway."

"Very good. I'll be there in a bit," replied Caroline. May be able to make some progress on things over the weekend after all, she thought as she got into her car.

---

Charlie Schreiber sat back in his rocking chair. Caroline had finished explaining her story. "I knew your granddaddy real good. We were buddies - played ball together, ran around chasing skirts even if he was three or four years older than me, before we both settled down. He told me all about the stuff written on his

188

granddaddy. He wanted it all destroyed. He was so god-damn disgusted with the stories about the church, how it came about, and what ol' Tom Weber had done. He just wanted it all out of his life."

"To him, it would be better if nobody knew anything about it, even if a lot of it was written in old German. There was an article from the Wamego newspaper way back that claimed that Thomas Weber had stolen money before leaving the old country. It told of what he had done with it. Andy, as he was known to everybody, was not happy that his granddaddy had wasted all the family money, filched or not, on churches."

"What?" blurted out Caroline, staring at the old man sitting across from her. "All the money on churches?"

"Why yes. Here is what your grandfather told me about Tom Weber."

The old man cleared his throat, then continued, "The word about him at the time was that he was dishonest, had come from the old country with a large amount of money that he had taken from investors. They said he had done it in advance of the collapse of the market for silver over there - he knew the drop was coming and cashed in before things got bad, leaving a lot of people high and dry. When he got over here, he bought every piece of land he could get his hands on. He had always denied the money was begotten illegally or anything of the sort. Anyway, he bought a lot of land and a few years later, started selling it to build churches in the Bohemian communities of Kansas. He apparently did it for many of them. Don't ask me why."

After a pause, the elderly man continued, "Well, sometime around 1900 or so, as I remember from Andy, a newspaper in Wamego published a story that all those Bohemian Catholic churches that had been appearing in the countryside were paid for with money embezzled by Thomas Weber in the old country. Now, you must know there was a lot of discrimination against Catholics in those days. The Bohemians were generally poor, they didn't speak English, at least for a long time, and there was suspicion about how all of a sudden all these really solid beautiful stone Catholic churches were appearing out of nowhere across the state. The appearance of this article caused quite a stir, As a result, the Bohemian community around Flush did everything they could to hide, even destroy, all reference to the Weber money and the old man's financing of the churches. But the article was a killer for old Tom Weber. He died within three or four years, unable to discredit the story, broken by it. He had practically nothing when he died, except the piece of land he left to his children. Nobody wanted to deal with him in the last years of his life. Both his own son Francis, I think his name was, and then Andrew, your grandfather, were ashamed of all this, were unable to discredit it. The old man's story of the whole affair, written in German which Andy could not read, was in the man's papers when he died in 1905 or 1906 and for some reason were put in the files in the rectory. I guess many of the Bohemians put their papers in the care of the church and the parish priest. Later, in the 1920's, the priest of the time, upon learning of the nature of all this, moved to protect the reputation of the Bohemian Catholic community in the state. He sought, along with Andy and his father to have the records of all this destroyed. But the man who was charged with destroying them did not destroy them at all. He put them aside to be able to, as far as I could tell, blackmail the Weber family at the most opportune time. As caretaker, it was easy for him to hide things in the rectory. He never got around to doin' any of the blackmailin', though. Just before he died in the early forties or so, he charged his son, who is a bit dimwitted, with the care of the rectory. Told him that no one was to be allowed to get into the archives, but I guess never told him about blackmailing the Webers. In any case, he would not have been smart enough to do any of that. When Father Biehler died in the early '70's, no priest replaced him, the church closed and the caretaker's son who lives down in Wabaunsee was the only one to have access to the old rectory. He is apparently a reclusive old man who gets along with no one, and is like I said, a bit loose in the head."

"I know. I found that out today. I went to see him. Scared me off with a couple of shotgun blasts. I will have to have Father Frank from the church in Wamego come with me next time," interjected Caroline.

"Not surprised." The old man paused a moment, then continued, "Young lady, you do need to get into that old place and see what's in there. Andrew thought it was all disposed of. Well, it wasn't. I learned that it had not been disposed of years after Andrew passed away. Supposed to have been a fire that was to be put out before it engulfed the whole building, something like that. There was no fire at all. Most of the stuff is apparently in German, though. Andrew had seen it all and he told me there was a lot about his grandfather and grandmother and their families that he couldn't understand. He just wanted it done away with. He was so mad that the old man had peed away, excuse the language, a fortune, in his mind anyway, on churches. Andrew was not wealthy by any means. He had a lot of trouble makin' ends meet during the thirties and after that, just like a lot of folks around here."

Caroline was incredulous. "Money on churches. And many of them, it appears."

"Oh, yes. I guess there were a few. Like I said, I think you should try to get into that old building and see what's there. And if you can, have somebody along who can read German."

"Whew," exhaled Caroline. "This is something, Mr. Schreiber, really something." She gently shook her head, and then continued, "I will definitely get into that old building and I believe I will have someone along who can read German writing." Caroline rose to leave.

"You can call me Charlie, young lady. And you say hello to your daddy. I haven't seen him in a while. We used to bring our hogs to the livestock auction in Onaga and I would sometimes

192

see him there. Been awhile. He probably doesn't raise hogs anymore."

"I will do that, Mr. Schreiber, and no, he doesn't raise hogs now - only cattle. I thank you very much for seeing me. Much obliged."

"Quite alright. You take care," he replied as Caroline left.

"Daddy, I am going to have some story to tell when this is over," said Caroline as she walked through the door of the farmhouse into the living room.

"I don't want to hear about it until you're done. It's been painful for the family all these years, although I really don't know why. Just that it was painful for my dad and his dad. All a long time ago, but I'm glad you are engaged in it. You have a right to know," replied Raymond Weber. He got up from watching the football game on TV and walked to the dining room for the traditional Weber family Sunday dinner. A dinner like many shared by many Kansas families of the time, of fried chicken with mashed potatoes, creamed corn and hot biscuits.

"Daddy, you know that Lucas, the young man I met in Vienna, will be here in two weeks. I think you will like him. I certainly do hope you hit it off. I like Lucas a lot, as I believe you and Mom know by now." Caroline was priming her dad. She knew he was leery of the boyfriends of his only daughter, his only child. She wanted the visit to go well.

"Well, have you figured this out yet, my dear?" replied Raymond Weber as he passed along the bowl of mashed potatoes. "I mean, just how serious is this new romance?"

"I like Lucas very much. We just met a little over a month ago, though. I don't know how far it's going to go. He is over there, and I am over here. We had a great time together in Europe."

"You're in love, aren't you?" smiled her father as he looked across the dining room table.

"Yes, I am, Daddy. I hope you like him." Caroline was beaming.

Raymond Weber had known for a long time his only child would most probably not want to continue the Weber farming tradition. He had hoped Caroline would find and marry a young man to whom he could turn over the farm. It was not to be, and he had known it for some time. Perhaps if she had gone to Kansas State - farm boys go there, but she had to go to KU - a pity. Farm boys don't go to KU.

"Well, I hope I do too. I just hope you don't go off and leave us here, half a world away." Raymond Weber tilted his head down to peer at his daughter over his glasses. "Does he like football, Caroline?"

"Yes, he does, but it's the English version, I'm afraid. We call it soccer here."

Caroline's mother, Lorraine, had been anticipating this discussion all weekend and had decided to keep quiet. She was

194

staying out of the discussion, at least for the time being. She knew how much Caroline liked the young Englishman. She had never seen her daughter so energetic and cheery over a young man before. The two were close. Caroline kept few secrets from her mother and Lorraine knew that her husband realized that as well. Raymond Weber looked over at his wife of twenty five years, who was having trouble holding back a smile. "You're pretty much OK with this, my dear?" Raymond Weber asked his wife with a wry smile on his face.

"Oh, we'll see," chortled Lorraine as she rose to return to the kitchen to refill the pitcher of water.

"We'll see, huh? You two have got this all figured out," chuckled Raymond as he observed the female complicity that had always succeeded in getting its way in his home. A man's home is his castle only as long as the women let it be that way, he thought.

---

Elizabeth spoke up as she and her son were finishing their after-dinner tea. "I spoke with Greta today. We had a nice chat. Karl had spent a few days in Zurich and had spoken with Claudia the other day as well. According to him, she was in good spirits. Things were apparently on the up and up with André. They had spent time in the Czech Republic in August. Had a great trip, saw a lot of castles in Prague and elsewhere and did the full tourist thing, according to Karl. You were probably there around the same time."

Lucas straightened up in his chair. "Mum, did you say Prague? André and Claudia were in Prague?"

"Why yes, it was Prague. A lot of other places as well. Why?"

"No, nothing. Just surprised they were there. Been there twice myself over the past few weeks. A funny coincidence". Lucas had a foreboding thought, but kept it to himself. Could André know anything about Dada's brother? Did he visit the museum? He must certainly know all about his family and their disappearance. If I know a lot about them now - it was pretty easy - he could very well know far more than I - it was his family, after all. Would he know anything about Helmut Bendt and who he was? I don't like the thought of this. There's the dispute about the inheritance, as well. It's not going away. Dada's getting pressure from them. Could all this get ugly?

Lucas rose, picked up the remaining dishes on the table, brought them to the kitchen, then went to the living room where he placed a call to the island.

Erik Brandt answered the phone, with an energetic *"Ja. Erik ist hier."*

"Dada, how are you?" a relieved Lucas Brandt asked his grandfather.

"Why, I am fine, Lucas. Anna's daughter and her husband were here for a few days and just left this morning. We had a

196

lovely time. And, the time is good now for some fishing. I plan to do a bit of that in the days to come. And how are you? When are you starting the job in Vienna again?" asked Erik.

"November 1. Looking forward to it. I'm glad to hear you are OK, as always. I said I would be in more frequent contact with you. Delivering on the promise. I must tell you, though, that I will be going to DC in a couple of weeks and then on to Kansas for a few days before going to Vienna. Once I get started a bit there, I will be down to see you." Lucas was not going to tell his grandfather about the source of his anxiety. Nothing happening - so far anyway. *Am I over-reacting to the news about André and Claudia being in Prague?*

"Ah, you are going to Kansas. Only one reason for that. Smitten you are, my dear Lucas. She must be worthy for you to travel all that way," chided the old man.

"I'm afraid so, I must admit. Maybe run into Toto over there. A part of America I don't know. In any case, you take care, and give my regards to Giuseppe. *Auf wiedersehen, Dada*." Lucas hung up the phone and made a mental note to call Giuseppe at his shop in the morning.

**The next day**

"Giuseppe, this is Lucas. How are you?"

"Well, I am doing remarkably well, *il mio amico*. To what can I attribute this call? You were just here," replied the elderly Italian.

"I need you to look after my grandfather for me. Check up on him from time to time. He is getting on, you know. Can I ask you to do that? I could ask the housekeeper to do that as well, but I understand she spends a lot of time with her family on the mainland and is not always around. Could you please make a point to knock on his door every other day or so? I would appreciate it very much."

"Well, certainly. I will do that. I see your grandfather just about every day already, but I will make a point of it. So, young man, when will I see you again?" asked the old man.

"Soon, Giuseppe, soon. I will be going to America in a few days, but will be starting work in Vienna in a month's time. I will be closer to be able to go see you. We will have a glass of Chianti on the square before you know it. You, grandfather, and I. I will try to call you regularly in the meantime. *Arrivederci*."

Lucas felt better, but he knew that the nagging thought of André possibly being aware of what he himself knew was not going to go away. The devastating connection he had discovered in the lives of his grandfather and of his aunt's husband was too livid to easily put into any recesses of his mind.

# Chapter 21

**Marseille, Friday morning, October 15 1999**

"Claudia, I need to drive to Rome today. I have some meetings lined up tomorrow with a buyer. He said Saturday morning was the best time for him and if he liked the material, we could meet again on Monday to finalize things, so I may have to stay over until Monday or Tuesday. I'm taking the Peugeot as I need to bring a number of samples. I will call you to let you know if I have to stay over. Going to the office now to pick up the samples and will then be on my way. It's close to a nine hour drive." André was lying. He had other plans. He had a meeting planned, but it wasn't in Rome, and it wasn't about blouses and shirts.

"OK," replied Claudia, as she pondered visiting one of her friends for a day or so if André was going to be away. "Drive safely. Italians are crazy on the road."

# Chapter 22

**Kansas, the day before**

Caroline had a plan for Lucas' stay. He would be arriving on Thursday a little after 5. They would have dinner at a restaurant on The Plaza, spend the night at her apartment and leave the next day for Westmoreland and the farm. They would spend the afternoon and evening with her parents with a horseback ride thrown in somewhere along the way, then drive to Lawrence on Saturday to see the football game with some of her friends. It's what people do in Kansas on Saturday afternoons in the fall, she thought. They'll do some tailgating with a tour of the campus where she had just spent four years of her life. Caroline had arranged with Father Frank that they would go to see Mr. Seitz after Mass at noon on Sunday. He had told her he had spoken with Clarence a few days after her unwanted visit. The old man had reluctantly agreed to lend them the keys to the Flush rectory if they came for them on Sunday and returned them by 6 PM that evening.

She and Lucas would drive back to Kansas City on Sunday night. Her boss had given her the OK to take that Monday off as well to complete the move of her things to Kansas City. Lucas would have to be at the airport at 4 PM on Monday for his flight back to London through JFK.

Caroline had difficulty in containing her excitement at the airport that Thursday afternoon. Just the same, she was wondering if her affection for him had just been a summer fling. Was it real? She was anxious to find out. It had been two months since they had seen each other, although they had spoken on the phone a number of times.

Leaving the narrow reception area and entering the walkaround corridor of the circular terminal, Lucas was literally jumped on by the young blond woman with a big smile from ear to ear, wrapping her arms around his neck.

"So glad you are here. Seems like forever." She kissed Lucas on the cheek and held him tight. She paused a moment, then continued "I can't believe I feel this way about someone after spending just a few days with him on the other side of the world. But it's true. So happy you are here." Caroline was wiping tears from her face and looking up at the object of her affection while holding his two hands in hers.

"I'm glad to be here, too. Really glad. Looking forward to making the most of it." Lucas bent over and kissed Caroline on the forehead, then held her to him for a moment. "So, show me

Kansas." He had the same questions in his mind as Caroline had in hers. *Was this real?*

As they left the airport, Caroline went over the plans she had made and Lucas filled her in on what had been happening in his life since they had last seen each other. He did not, however, mention anything about the activities around his research into his aunt's husband's family - the Gralla connection, the Jewish Museum in Prague, the Holocaust research. Nor of the anxiety for his grandfather that had been lurking in his mind for weeks and which had dominated his thoughts during the flight that day.

"So, how do your parents feel about this Englishman coming all this way to see their daughter, staying with her at her apartment and then spending the weekend with them?" Lucas was being mischievous, but there was truth in the question for him.

"They are OK with this. Daddies will be daddies. Prepare yourself for scrutiny. He's a craggy-faced leather-skinned tough middle-aged rancher who has been pretty successful in business and in judging men over the course of his life. But he has a big heart and wants me to be happy. He would like me to find an energetic farm-boy agricultural college graduate who knows the difference between heifers and steers and wears cowboy boots like him for me to spend my life with, but he knows that is probably not going to happen. The real key is my mother. She is happy to see me happy about this. As she goes, so will my Dad. She will like you, I am sure, British accent and all. In any case,

Lucas, we've just met. Let's enjoy the weekend. It will be all right."

An hour later, Lucas and Caroline entered the restaurant on Kansas City's elegant Spanish-style Plaza compound and found a table in the corner.

"Lucas, I forgot to tell you. Marcela the researcher in Plzen informed me that the name of my great-great-grandmother, the wife of Thomas Weber, was really Barbara-Louisa Cobourg-Strauss and not just Barbara Strauss. No wonder we couldn't find anything. She had dropped the Cobourg. She was born in the town of Ronsperg. Marcela found their marriage record in the files of a parish church in Prague. No wonder..." Lucas interrupted what she was saying."What did you say?" shaking his head abruptly in wonderment of what he had just heard. "Her family name was Cobourg-Strauss and she was from Ronsperg?" His mouth was open. "I can't believe this… incredible."

"What's incredible? You look like you've seen a ghost. I have the right name of my great-great-grandmother now. What's so incredible about that?"

Lucas straightened up in his chair and let out a low whistle, then answered. "Caroline, this is going to be a long story. It looks like our families are connected. I have a Cobourg-Strauss in my family as well..... Yes, a Cobourg-Strauss and from Ronsperg, as well, I am afraid. It is complicated and I have only been aware of it all in the last month or so."

Caroline was incredulous across the table. "What? We could be related somehow already?"

"No. It doesn't go that far. We're not related by blood. It's not that. Let me explain. Maybe we had better order first." Lucas nervously signaled for the waiter and they proceeded to order their meals with a glass of wine, per the suggestion of the waiter. *I'm going to need it,* thought Lucas, as he prepared to tell the story of his aunt Claudia.

Lucas continued what he had started. Not many people know this. You must be careful with what I am going to tell you. I don't really feel all right in telling you this, but the family connection is too incredible for me to keep it to myself. Please, Caroline, this is pretty sensitive stuff." Caroline nodded. He proceeded to her the story of Claudia.

"This was all told to me by my grandfather when I visited him after you returned home in August. There are other elements my grandfather told me about his own family that are of concern to me these days, but that is something else. The Cobourg-Strauss family I am talking about is most assuredly the Cobourg-Strauss family in your own ancestry. Ronsperg, now Pobezovice, Bohemia, is and always has been a very small town. There was only one extended Cobourg-Strauss family, I am pretty certain, and they had apparently owned just about everything for miles around."

"Wow." Caroline was wide-eyed and simply staring at Lucas. After a brief pause, she dropped her head and blurted "this is incredible, Lucas. I don't know what to say. But it may have a happy ending. Let me explain." Lucas was not sure about the happy ending, but there was no way Caroline could know, yet anyway, what his current anxiety was all about.

Caroline continued. "With the results from Marcela and what I have been delving into here, I am in the process of getting closer to the real story of my own family and of my great-great-grandfather, Thomas Weber, from Ronsperg. The village of Mutenin where he was born is three kilometers down the road from Ronsperg. I am getting access to some papers on him on Sunday, by the way, and you are going to be with me. The papers, which have been hidden away for a long time are all in German. I will need you to tell me what they say. This is all pretty amazing, Lucas - a real Bohemian Connection. Maybe the papers in the files will shed light on the Cobourg-Strauss family - after all, Thomas Weber was married to one. This is so funny." Caroline was close to laughing. She paused a moment, then continued, "Now that we are on the subject of my ancestry search, which brought us together in the first place, you may remember what I told you about my findings in Vienna - that my great-great-grandfather was a banker there but had come from Bohemia. Well, I have discovered that all the land he bought here in Kansas with the money he apparently took out of Austria before the Crash was sold a number of years later. It was used to pay for a dozen or more Catholic churches for the many Bohemian communities that sprang up across Kansas in the

1870's and 1880's. Succeeding generations of my family have been upset about that for close to a century, although my dad doesn't really care by now. I was told by an old friend of my father's father who I saw two weeks ago that the papers should shed light on the whole story of the Bohemian churches and Thomas Weber's paying for them. Getting access to them has had its own intrigue, by the way. Hot stuff, really. I got shot at trying to get at the material. Well, not really shot at, but close to it. Tell you all about it in Westmoreland" Caroline looked across at Lucas and with a wry smile on her face, said "So, I'm related to your aunt Claudia, but not to you."

"Looks that way. Quite amazing." Lucas had a smile as well, but lurking in the back of his mind was the condition of his Dada. He had called him from Washington before getting on the plane but there was no answer. Maybe he was out fishing. He said he would be doing that these days. Out in a boat on a calm sea at the end of day. His favorite pastime. He had been unable to reach Giuseppe. It was evening in Italy and the shop was closed.

Caroline giggled. "This is incredible, truly incredible."

"You have to promise me, Caroline. Nobody else knows about my aunt. My grandfather would be devastated if he knew I shared this with you. A promise?"

"A promise."

The waiter arrived with their food and their talk took another direction. "You haven't told me much about the job with the research foundation. How is it? Is it what you thought it would be?" Lucas asked.

"Not really. I'm a bit disappointed. The place is far more political than I thought and certainly of more of a philosophical bent to the right than I had thought before I started. It's kind of a think tank for the Republican Party and next year, being an election year, the office is doing a lot of work for Republican candidates at the federal and state levels. I'm not too enthused about that. My dad is a Republican and makes no bones about it, but I am more liberal, and that term is not a popular one in my state. Kansas is Republican country." Lucas, across the table, decided that he was not going to tell Caroline just yet that he was a Tory supporter back home. Before he could say anything, she teasingly asked, "Think you can find me a job in Vienna? I'm not sure I can last all that long with all the Bush for President people around me."

Lucas laughed, but was not entirely sure it was a hypothetical question. "We'll see. Let me get there first." They finished their meal and, looking forward to spending the night together, rose and left the restaurant.

The next morning, Caroline woke first and gazed at the young man next to her she was falling even more in love with. After three or four minutes, Lucas opened his eyes, turned his head to see Caroline propped on her elbow two feet away staring at him. "I am becoming serious about it, Lucas. Do you think I could find a job in Vienna?" as she ran her index finger slowly across his chest.

Lucas turned, put his arms around Caroline and kissed her on the forehead, followed by "I think that would be an excellent idea. There are many international organizations in Vienna. I will look into it, although getting an EU working permit may be a chore. But......yes! Let me look into it when I get there," as he kissed Caroline, ran his hand over her hip and drew her to him, and thought to himself that he would like that very much.

# Chapter 23

Lucas and Raymond Weber got along just fine, right from the start. This despite the wizened old rancher's question to Lucas within an hour of their meeting, with Caroline momentarily not present, if the young man was going to take his daughter away from them, from Kansas, and from their world.

Lucas did not hesitate in his response. "Mr. Weber, I don't know that right now. I really don't. But I understand your concern. I will always be frank with you. That you can count on, sir. I appreciate your daughter very much. We just met, though." He was not ready to tell his girlfriend's father that they were already talking about doing just that. *A lot had to happen first.*

"Young man, I appreciate your honesty. I look forward to knowing you more, assuming you continue to see each other. Welcome once again to the plains of Kansas and our pretty peaceful world out here. I hope we can make you like it and it makes you want to come back." Lorraine Weber had implored her husband to not be too hard on the young man who, clearly, was the object of their daughter's affections, more so than any other young man she had ever been involved with. Raymond reflected that Lorraine had little to worry about. He liked what he had seen so far. "Now, what do you do?" asked the elder of the two, as they sat in the living room of the large ranch-style house, waiting for Caroline to finish saddling up the horses for the ride around the property before dinner.

Lucas spoke about his approaching job with UNIDO as an industrial development economist and his three years with the World Bank on projects in Asia and Africa. "I basically work with developing countries to help them plan their most important economic infrastructure projects - transportation and energy supply, ports, railroads and other building blocks required for key industries that they have the basics to develop." Lucas spoke of a couple of examples of projects that he had worked on. Then Caroline arrived to say the horses were ready and hitched out front. It was time to see the farm.

They rode for an hour over hills of sandy colored grass blowing in the wind. They rode down through gullies and tree-lined creek beds that wound between the hills and the hundreds of grazing Weber Land and Livestock Company cattle in a scene that stretched in every direction as far as Lucas could see.

Lively discussions amongst Raymond, Caroline, her mother and Lucas continued around the dinner table that evening. Lucas talked about the German and English sides of his family, while his mind wandered occasionally to his grandfather back in Italy.

He made a point to ask Caroline if he could make a call to the island early in the morning.

There was no answer at the villa. Lucas then placed a call to Giuseppe's cobbler shop. The old man answered. "Giuseppe, this is Lucas. I am calling from America. I have been trying to reach my grandfather. Have you seen him today?"

"No, Lucas, I have not," replied the man. "I have not seen him for two days, as a matter of fact. I knocked on his door last evening, as I promised you I would, but there was no answer. I have not seen his vehicle for a couple of days either. I am afraid I have no news for you. Should we be worried? What is of concern to you, Lucas?"

"It is maybe nothing. It is just that he is getting old and I am a concerned grandson." Lucas was not about to share with him the real nature of his apprehensions. "I will call you again on Monday if you don't mind."

"Certainly. *Nessun problema. Arrivederci, giovane.*"

"And to you, Giuseppe."

Dada could just be travelling about somewhere. He loved to do it. Just the same.....

The following morning, Caroline and Lucas drove to Lawrence to see the Kansas Jayhawks' football game that afternoon with the visiting Oklahoma State Cowboys. Raymond had chided Lucas at breakfast about the latter's appreciation for soccer, which he said was the game little kids played in Kansas and elsewhere in the United States before they were old enough to try out for real football. Lucas chuckled at that.

They arrived in Lawrence late morning, took a quick walking tour of the tree-lined, sprawling campus and joined some college friends of Caroline for some beer and a tailgate meal in the parking lot behind the stadium before the game. The kick-off to the game was preceded by a crowd-raising rendition of the Jayhawk fight song. The uniformed University of Kansas marching band playing it strode down the field in 10 rows of trumpets, trombones, tubas, cymbals and drums, with majorettes with their twirling batons and strutting drum majors in huge fur hats leading it all. It culminated with the 50,000 fans singing the traditional school song of Rock Chalk Jayhawk. It was the first American college football game that Lucas had ever attended and he quickly understood why spectacles like this were so much a part of America. Nevertheless, he mused to himself that Liverpool and Manchester United on a Sunday afternoon back home at Old Trafford was every bit a comparable spectacle. English fans are crazier, though. After the game, Caroline, Lucas, and her friends found a table at The Wheel, the popular campus pub, downed a couple of pitchers of beer and ordered an early dinner of the house specialty of fried chicken in a basket before returning to the farm.

The next morning, Caroline and Lucas got into her car to follow her parents to Sunday Mass in Wamego. After Mass, Father Frank joined Caroline and Lucas to drive to Wabaunsee.

When they got to the Seitz place, no one was around. Not a soul. Tacked on the porch post nearest the front door was a piece of paper above a tin can. Father Frank got out of the car, retrieved the piece of paper with a note saying, in essence that the key to the rectory was in the can and that he had better bring it back. The priest chuckled, realizing that crazy old Clarence was most certainly watching them from some point unseen.

Father Frank, Caroline and Lucas then drove to where Flush had once been and where the church and rectory still stood. Lucas was struck by the solitary appearance of the two buildings, essentially in the middle of nowhere, sitting in a clump of trees, with fields all around. Across the highway was a cemetery with an old padlocked rusty gate with no apparent new graves, or flowers anywhere. Whatever community there had been around this church was long gone.

Father Kurtz crossed the little square in front of the old Bohemian church and approached the door of the rectory. He unlocked it and they entered into what was once a reception area. It smelled of old wood and mold. A thick layer of dust rested on the chairs along the wall, on the curved handrail of the stairway and on everything else as well. Off to the right was a door with the word for office in both Czech and German - *Kancelar / Buro*. Caroline took the key ring from Father Frank, jumbled with the keys until she found the right one for the door, and entered, followed by Lucas and Father Frank. Covering the inside wall of the room were a series of wooden cabinets, six drawers high with shelves on top leading to the high ceiling. The drawers were labeled alphabetically. A long metal bar ran the height of each line of drawers with a padlock at the top. Caroline quickly found the drawer with the letter W. She found the key for the padlock and unlocked it. Opening the drawer, she observed a bundle of documents held by a ribbon, a stack of six or seven thick leather folders with names on them - Petr Weiss, Johann Wacha, and other names. She took the large thick bundle and saw when turning it over, the name of Tomas Weber in German-style lettering.

"Here they are - the Weber papers. A whole bundle of stuff, it looks like."

The bundle contained ten to fifteen documents of different thickness and dimensions. The first document was an unsealed envelope that she opened and saw contained something written in German. She put it aside to see the other documents. One was a certificate of entry to the United States for a Thomas Weber, dated April 20, 1873, stating that the person was received at the City of New York, disembarking from the ship the Idaho which had arrived from Liverpool. A similar entry certificate was there for a Barbara Strauss Weber with the same information. A third document was a Certificate of Naturalization as a Citizen of the United States for Thomas Weber, dated October 15, 1887, then what looked to be Thomas Weber's will, dated November 2, 1903. There followed a stack held together by another ribbon of what appeared to be deeds of purchase and sale of land. Caroline undid the ribbon and saw, sorting quickly through the documents, the records of the purchase and sale of a good part, if not all, of the fourteen thousand acres of land that her great-great-grandfather had owned across north-central Kansas. Underneath that bundle was a page from an old newspaper that fell to the floor. Caroline picked it up. It was the front page of **THE WAMEGO REPORTER** of March 6, 1902.

The headline in big letters in two lines across the page read **Bohemian Churches in State Built with Stolen Money,** with the byline of *J.B. Newell, Publisher and Editor*.

"Lucas, Father Frank, look at this," as she quickly read the old front-page article.

> Kansans can now know where the Bohemian immigrant settlers across our beloved state found the money to pay for all of the nice Catholic churches that have been built in their communities over the past decade. The money was stolen. Thomas Weber, an immigrant land-owner now of Flush was a banker in Vienna before coming to this country in 1873. He brought with him many thousands of dollars that, it is reported, were stolen from investors before the Vienna Crash of 1873 which sent Europe into its prolonged economic depression. This newspaper has it from good sources that Mr. Weber escaped the difficulties in the old country just before the Crash, came to the United States with much illicit-gotten money from cheated investors in his pockets, and proceeded to buy thousands of acres of land across eastern Kansas. It is said that the generally destitute and poor Bohemians in our midst, knowing of Mr. Weber's wealth, never mind the means through which it was accumulated, convinced the latter to

provide the money for the construction of the twelve admittedly fine-looking stone Catholic churches of the communities of Blaine, Flush, Gorham, Timken, Pilsen and seven others at last count in our state. Mr. Weber has denied stealing any money from investors or any others in the old country or here in Kansas, but has not succeeded according to the authorities of the Catholic church in Leavenworth, in explaining to their satisfaction the source of the money for the construction of the churches. It is said that Mr. Weber's brother, a Jesuit priest at the Seminary at St. Marys, who had been discredited in his home country of Bavaria before coming to America, was highly influential in directing the financial resources of Mr. Weber to the construction of the churches. Sources have confirmed to this newspaper the depth of concern the church authorities have for the reputation of the Bohemian Catholic community in the state of Kansas as well as for the suspected questionable Jesuit involvement in the construction of the network of churches.

J.B.N.

Caroline let out a low barely audible whistle as she finished reading the piece, which had apparently condemned her great-great-grandfather to disgrace and an ignominious end to his life.

"Boy, this certainly could have done it for old Thomas," she said as she looked at Father Frank and Lucas. "Let's see what the document in German says. Lucas, need you for this."

Lucas began to read the German writing and relay to Caroline and Father Frank what it said.

"OK, C. This is something signed by Thomas Weber, as I can see on the last page. It is probably twenty pages long, but looks quite legible. Do I read this now or do we bring it to the farm?" asked Lucas.

"Read it now. I can't wait any longer. Father Frank, are you OK with that?"

"Yes, of course," said the priest. "Let's do it. I am curious about this as well. Go ahead."

"Ok, here goes," said Lucas.

My name is Thomas Weber. I was born Tomas Weber in 1828 in Mutenin, Bohemia. My father was Johann Weber, a peasant from the German-speaking village of Mutenin and my mother Anna Pavec, from the nearby Czech village of Sibanov. I was raised in the languages of both my parents, although my schooling, however brief it was, was in German and the language I am most comfortable in writing to this day. We were a family of four children, two of which, a brother and a sister both older than I, died in childhood. I do not remember them. My surviving brother Peter was ordained a priest in the Jesuit order in Bavaria, satisfying the wishes of my parents, and accompanied my own family and I to America in 1873.

This is my story. I am writing it in my 77th year for the benefit of my family and my fellow Bohemians who have followed me to this great country. They deserve to understand what I have done with my life, the actions I have taken since coming here, and why.

At the age of 10, soon after the deaths of both of my parents, I terminated my schooling at the school run by the priests in nearby Hostau and began a period of 25 years of service to the masters of the domain of Ronsperg, of which my home village of Mutenin was part. The domain was the property of the Cobourg-Strauss family, who had it in their family since the 1600's. The source of the family's considerable wealth, was the rich deposits of silver and quartz throughout the land and the sale of those minerals to the governments and royal families of Europe, particularly that of the Austrian Empire. It was in those mines that I began my working life. It was hard work for young peasant men like me, particularly Czech, who had little opportunity to work at anything else. At the age of seventeen I was promoted by the lord of the Cobourg-Strauss family and master of the domain, to foreman in the principal silver mine of the estate. This had a lot to do with the fact that I could read and write German, which none of the uneducated Czech mine workers could do. In the same year, I made the acquaintance of Barbara Louisa, my future wife, the daughter of the brother of the master of the domain. We fell in love and, over the objections of her family - I was from the peasant class, of mixed German and Czech heritage and she of the nobility on the Austrian side - were married in a small ceremony in Prague two years later. We were both 19 years of age. I managed to be accepted once again in time by the master of the domain and succeeded within a few years to be made manager of the business affairs of the estate, working closely with my wife's brother, who represented the interests of the family business in Prague. The master of the domain of the time, Count Rudolf Cobourg-Strauss, had become increasingly removed from the operations of the family businesses, being closely involved with the Vienna court as an advisor to the emperor, Franz Josef, who is still emperor to this day.

Over the following fifteen years, until the fateful year of 1862, I managed to expand the Cobourg-Strauss silver mining business, accumulating for myself as well a not inconsiderable degree of wealth with the acknowledgement and consent of the Cobourg-Strauss family. The operations of the silver mining and smeltering business was the principal source of the wealth of the family, allowing them to do what they wanted to do, enjoy the favor of the court, and I was the overseer of it.

The problems that led to my leaving the employ of the Ronsperg estate and of the Cobourg-Strauss family had to do with the activities of my brother-in-law, Frederick, operating on behalf of the family businesses in Prague. In 1860, over the wishes of his uncle Rudolf, the head of the family, and of my own reservations, Frederick began selling large quantities of silver to the Jewish metals merchants of Prague. This was causing problems for the head of the family with the court of the Emperor. Members of the court accused the family of destabilizing the currency through clandestine sales. Too much silver was coming into circulation. A further complication of this was that, known to Frederick but not to me at the time, the Jewish money traders were in turn selling much of the silver they were buying to the government of Prussia, which was becoming the principal enemy of the Austrian Empire. Prussia, like Austria, had silver as the underpinning of its currency. Cobourg-Strauss sales of silver to Prussia through the Jewish money traders of Prague were solidifying the economic underpinnings of Austria's increasingly avowed enemy. The two countries, as the world knows, eventually went to war in 1866.

If the scion of the family, was to continue to enjoy the favor of the Emperor and wield influence at court - he had been named ambassador to a number of courts of Europe by the Emperor over the previous decade - this could not continue. Frederick, on the other hand, was determined to advance the business interests of the family as well as accumulate a sizable fortune for himself, uncle Rudolf's objections and influence at court in his way or not. Despite this, he was much loved by the other members of the family, including my wife, Barbara.

In the spring of 1862, Count Rudolf Cobourg-Strauss called a meeting of the family at Ronsperg Castle to discuss the matter. The meeting turned ugly. Rudolf, whose temper was legendary, ended up taking his nephew Frederick by the collar to the window on the third floor of the castle and throwing him out to his death on the cobblestones below. His neck was broken and so was the family. Defenestration they called it in the old country, a particularly Bohemian manner of dealing with disputes.

Lucas' thoughts turned to what Caroline and he had learned in the Czech Republic about people being thrown from windows. Defenestration they all call it. The one in Prague starting the Thirty Years' War, the one two hundred years before that, the one with the Czech leader Masaryk being thrown out of a window of a palace after the war...This one....Very strange stuff, this practice." Lucas continued the reading.

This was not the first defenestration involving the Cobourg-Strauss family. An ancestor of my wife's family was thrown from the third floor of Prague Castle in 1618, triggering the bloody Thirty Years war. Strangely enough, a survivor of that incident ceded the domain of Ronsperg to the line of the Austrian family that my wife was part of."

Yes, thought Lucas. The Cobourg-Strauss connection with his own aunt, but also connected to the famous incident in Prague. This is new..... Ronsperg ceded to a Cobourg-Strauss as a result of that incident....

"Caroline, I am learning stuff here about connections to my own family, what we discussed the other night in Kansas City. Quite unbelievable. It all goes back to Prague and 1618." Lucas looked at Father Frank apologetically, "Forgive us, Father. Something about a member of my own family being connected to the family of Mr. Weber's wife somewhere along the line. It would be a long story."

"No problem, young man. Just continue with this here. I don't need to know all about the other connections, however incredible they may be," replied Father Frank.

Lucas continued.

As a result of this incident at the Castle, I decided to leave the estate and the employ of the family. I could not continue to work with or for, Count Rudolf Cobourg-Strauss. Barbara did not object to this decision. Frederick was her favorite brother. They had grown up together. She was disconsolate and enraged with her uncle, who was never arrested or prosecuted for the crime. Such were the prerogatives of the nobility of the time. The Count was not happy with my decision to leave the employ of the family but did nothing to stop me. He had become disenchanted with my influence with the workers and the other peasants of the estate. He was also resentful of my increasing wealth as a merchant of much of the output of the mines, despite the considerable royalties paid to the estate on such. He soon afterwards named his own son as head of the business operations of the domain.

As I mentioned earlier in this narrative, I had managed to accumulate a respectable sum of personal wealth as manager of the family mining business and would use it to enter business in Vienna. As well, Barbara had inherited a considerable sum of money from her mother's side of the family, which added to our financial security. In late 1862, Barbara, our children Franz and Marghareta and I left Ronsperg for Vienna, where I found an opportunity to buy a share in the partnership of a merchant banking firm. The firm had a seat on the Wiener Borse, the stock exchange of the realm. It was at this time that I began to write my name as Thomas Weber. The German version would be better for conducting business in Vienna. The firm I bought into provided financing to importers and manufacturers in Austria, and to wealthy individuals who speculated in railroad stocks and silver mines, the latter being something I knew a lot about. I thrived in the banking business and managed with my partners to grow the firm from 10 employees when I joined to over 70 a few years later. However, I could see clouds on the horizon. Soon after the end of the Franco-Prussian war of 1870-71, the chancellor of Prussia decided to take that country off the silver standard. It would be simply a matter of time before prices of silver would plunge, taking many businesses and financial houses with them. A panic could very well ensue. I decided to leave the banking business before the panic came, as I knew it would. In late 1872, I sold my share in the firm to my partners who did not share the same pessimism and made plans to go to America. It was time to leave what I saw as the turbulence and decay of a corrupt Europe and embrace the opportunity of America. Barbara agreed. She had become disenchanted with her family and was increasingly estranged from the other members living back in Bohemia. On her papers for emigration to America, she wrote her name as Barbara Strauss Weber, leaving out the Cobourg part of it. From that point forward, Cobourg was no longer part of my wife's name.

In the meantime, my brother Peter, who was a teacher in Munich, was thrown out of Germany in 1872 with all the other Jesuits there by the Chancellor, von Bismarck, and had come to live in Vienna. Upon learning of my decision to emigrate, he decided to do the same given the persecution of the Jesuits at that time. He accompanied us on our voyage to this country the following year.

Upon arriving in America, I had no intention of continuing as a banker or financier. For one, I could not speak English and even if I could, conditions were hardly better for people in the banking business in America at that time. I decided to go to the Midwest, where there were other Germans and Czech-speaking Bohemians, buy whatever land I could and get into business, with the nature of such to be determined. I arrived in Kansas in the summer of 1873 and settled the family, at least temporarily, in Wamego. I proceeded over the next three years to buy up as much land as I had the means to afford around Wamego and elsewhere in northeast Kansas while building a farm supply business with a local partner who had emigrated from Bohemia a number of years before. This partner, Marek Kravek, did most of the work at least in the early years, as I knew little about the farming business, while I provided the financial support and management to make it a success. In the meantime, I had chosen a section of my land holdings for my own family, a 160 acre plot I had purchased not far from the village of Flush, a few miles north of Wamego. It is where I live as I write this narrative. Over the next fifteen years, the business did quite well, and at the age of 62 in 1890, I decided to retire from active involvement and sold my share to my partner.

It was in that year that I decided to assist the immigrant Bohemian community in building churches in their communities. Ever since I had arrived in the Midwest in the 1870's, I had deplored the difficult circumstances of my fellow Bohemian Catholics in practicing their faith. Whatever churches there were, were generally of poor construction. Masses were often carried out in open fields or in buildings built for other purposes. Furthermore, there was and still is general discrimination against the Czech speaking Bohemians across Kansas, and particularly those of the Catholic faith, which represents the vast majority of the Bohemians. Irish and German Catholics have been discriminated against as well. My brother Peter, the Jesuit priest, was by 1890 one of the longest serving priests of the Jesuit Mission and Seminary at St. Marys, not far from Wamego. He influenced me greatly in my decision to provide the money for the building of proper churches for the Bohemian communities across Kansas. The first one was the one in Flush not far from the section where I live today, a fine sandstone structure with a beautiful interior, and in whose rectory I have entrusted this memoir. Over the next decade, eleven other Catholic churches were built with my financial backing, in Blaine, Pilsen, Gorham, and other Bohemian Catholic communities identified as being in need by Peter and his fellow priests.

It was something noble that I wanted to do. I had made a lot of money in my life and I didn't need to have or keep any more than I needed to live. My beloved wife Barbara had died suddenly in 1886. I had little use of all of the land that I had bought since coming to Kansas, over fourteen thousand acres, which in any case was not appreciating in value during the depression of the early '90's. So, I decided to pay for the construction of the churches by selling off pieces of my land holdings, piecemeal as funds were required. I did this over an eight year period, which turned out to be one of the finest periods of my life. I worked closely with the various communities and their priests in the planning and construction of their churches. We insisted on the employment of the young Bohemian men in the communities in their construction. I am proud of what we did. The Bohemian Catholic communities of Kansas, most of them anyway, have a proper place of worship and a source of communal pride. I must say, however, that I dismayed my own children in this activity, with them resenting my use of my land holdings for this purpose, despite my willing to them of over a thousand acres of the choice sections I owned around Westmoreland. I regret that this is the case. It is also the reason I have left this narrative in the hands of my good friend and parish priest of St. Joseph of Flush, as a record of the truth regarding the Bohemian churches of Kansas.

This brings me to the unfortunate part of this story and with which the most recent years of my life have taken a distressing turn.

As mentioned earlier in this narrative, there was and still is much discrimination and prejudice against the immigrant Bohemian community and Catholics in general in Kansas. Furthermore, although this was not the intent, there was resentment in many of the communities with Bohemian populations that the churches that I paid for with my own money were generally larger and more impressive in their construction than the other local churches. For one, most of the Protestant ones were made of wood with a simple frame while the Bohemian churches were of stone, in the style of European village churches that the immigrant community wished to emulate. This resentment as well as the general disbelief, I concede, that someone would use practically all of his wealth to build a dozen churches for communities where he does not even live has led people to doubt, to question, the motives and the source of the funds of Thomas Weber in this decade-long endeavor of mine. Many of the Kansas Bohemians have been grateful, but many have been skeptical of my motives and of the source of the money. I had been a wealthy mine operator on behalf of a rich estate owner and had been a banker, whereas virtually all of the Bohemian immigrants to Kansas were peasants and small craftsmen in their home country. They saw me as coming from a totally different world, although our roots and family heritages were similar. The resentment of me in this regard combined with the general prejudice of the majority Protestant community against Bohemian Catholics culminated with the appearance two years ago of a front-page article written by the publisher of the Wamego Reporter. It was reproduced in papers in a number of other communities in Kansas with Bohemian populations, declaring that the funds used for the construction of the various Bohemian Catholic churches across Kansas built in the 1890's were stolen. Stolen by me in my capacity as a banker in the old country before coming to America. Nothing could be further from the truth. The money came from my hard work of over fifty years, starting as a mine laborer, then rising to be placed in charge of the commercial activities of one of the principal estates of Bohemia, then building one of the most successful and respected merchant banking firms in Vienna, all without stealing a pfennig from anyone. I suppose people could suspect me of some sort of wrong-doing by my leaving the banking business just prior to the Crash in 1873. But I could see the difficulties coming and sold my shares to my partners, who did not share my pessimism about the state of the economy of the Austrian Empire. I was fortunate to have the foresight, but I did not cheat or steal anything from anyone in the process of leaving the banking business of Vienna. My family may resent what I have done for the Bohemians of Kansas, but I am proud of my actions and have no regrets.

The newspaper article of two years ago has caused me great distress. Despite my poor health, I have sought diligently to rectify the facts. I have spoken at a number of churches to parishioners about the truth of my activities. The myth nevertheless persists and I am weary of speaking of it. I know in my mind what I have done, the good that I have provided, and such is sufficient for my piece of mind. I am not well right now. I entrust the truth of all this to my priest and confessor.

Thomas Weber, April 1904.

Caroline had been sitting on the corner of the desk. The reading had taken close to thirty minutes, as Lucas took pains to faithfully translate the German text. Father Frank had found an old upholstered swivel chair on coasters in the corner and had sat transfixed as Lucas read to them the words of the aging German-Czech Bohemian gentleman who had tried to do what he could for his poor brethren in America and had been vilified for it. She spoke first. "This is a tragic story. All he wanted to do was help, to give them pride, decent places to worship and centers for their community activities."

"Yes, it is tragic, I must say," interjected the priest. "I wonder how that myth got started. He doesn't say, does he, Lucas?"

"No, nothing about that, as far as I can tell," replied Lucas.

"We will probably never know the source of it. But it is unfortunate," interjected Caroline. "He had the money to do it, so he did it. I suppose the common Bohemian immigrant from peasant stock was so used to being manipulated and cheated in the old country that he believed the rumor and the myth, and my ancestor could not convince him otherwise."

Caroline then picked up the document that appeared to be Thomas Weber's will. It was not a long one. It was simply a letter addressed to a C.L. Sullivan, Attorney, describing what was to be ceded to Francis Weber and Margaret Weber Dekat - his children, thought Caroline. The plots of land and other items of value, including his wife's jewelry. There was no mention of any other properties. Caroline paused a moment, then said "This is the end for me in this. I have discovered what I needed to know. The truth is reassuring. I look forward to sharing all this with my father. Father Frank, will it cause the parish, the diocese, or whoever else, any problems if I take these papers out of here and bring them home? I think they deserve to be with our family. Do you agree?"

"Caroline, you can do what you wish with these papers. They are yours. Old Clarence Seitz may raise a fuss, but he has no say in this. I will not even tell him about it. Take them, please."

Lucas was silent as they left the rectory. His thoughts were on the remarkable convergence of the histories of Caroline's family and that of the bloodline of his aunt Claudia. An incredible and improbable Bohemian Connection. And another story of someone being thrown out of a window.

Later, at dinner, Caroline outlined to her parents everything she had learned. She showed them the documents from the rectory, the will, the newspaper article, the letter in German, the deeds of purchase and sale, everything.

Her father had listened intently to everything. "Well, I must say, my dear, I am very glad you have done this. It puts the past of the family in a very different light. My daddy and his daddy stayed away from this. I discouraged you from getting into it, as you know. Everybody around here thought we descended from an old-world thief who dishonored the Bohemians. As I think about it, I just may want to bring the truth to the attention of what remains of the community. This changes things. Our heritage here becomes something else. I just may do it. Need to think about it. Father Frank was there today, right? I think I'll go see him. And soon."

Talk around the table regarding Thomas Weber's letter to his descendants continued for another half-hour. Caroline and her mother retired to the kitchen after clearing the table. Raymond invited Lucas outside for a walk across the road to check on a sick foal.

Lucas took advantage of the absence of the ladies to speak as they walked up the path to the barn. "Mr. Weber, I have thoroughly enjoyed my stay with you and Mrs. Weber this weekend. I now understand a great deal more about this part of the world, which I knew very little about before, and to which I admit I could become attached. There is a friendly, earnest, down to earth energy, yet reassuring stability of life here."

Raymond looked over with a smile on his face as they walked. Lucas continued. "It is very different from the complicated and heavily regulated life of Europe with upheaval seemingly constantly around the corner. I am quite fond of your daughter, as you probably realize. I don't know what the future holds for us. But I hope you understand that my intentions regarding your daughter are the most honorable."

The two men entered the horse barn with Raymond listening intently, as Lucas went on, looking at Raymond as he spoke. "I have never felt so strongly about someone before, Mr. Weber. We seem to be one and the same when we are together. I feel instinctively at ease with your daughter, who is very strong of character and lets one know what she thinks about things." Lucas paused a moment, then continued. "You must know something about me, however. I am at pains to tell you of it. Nevertheless, it is something you should know. Five months ago, I was in a jail in Singapore." Seeing the alarm on Raymond Weber's face, Lucas quickly continued. "Yes, a jail in Singapore, and an unwitting dupe of a scheme that I was not aware of. I was absolved of any wrong-doing, however, thanks to the efforts of my lawyer uncle and grandfather and the realization of the authorities there that I had been duped into what I was accused of, without my knowledge."

Raymond interjected. "Let's have a seat. This sounds like it could take awhile. The horses seem to be OK, at least for the next little while. You are not leaving until later," motioning to bales of hay that would serve as seating as Lucas related the story of the incident in Asia.

"I can assure you, Mr. Weber, that I have no record of any crime or anything of the sort. As proof of my innocence and clean record of behavior, I have been hired by an agency of the United Nations who looked into the incident and came to the conclusion, as did my employer at the time, the World Bank, that I had no part in any wrong-doing. Caroline has known all about this since the first days of our meeting in Vienna. I had asked her to not mention anything about it, but I believe it is right you should know this happened to me. It is not something I would wish upon my worst enemy. I hope you understand, sir, and not let it cloud your view of me."

"I am glad you told me this, Lucas. I believe you. I think I'm a pretty good judge of character. I believe my daughter is also. I decided the other night that what I saw of Lucas Brandt was pretty much the essence of what he was about." With a wry smile on his face, Raymond Weber nevertheless was not going to let the young man totally off the hook, "But, I can tell you, I will kick your ass from here to the Grand Canyon if I ever hear you doing anything to my daughter that would cause me alarm." The lean, rough-hewn rancher then put his arm around Lucas's shoulders. With a big smile on his face, he said "We'll see where this all goes. Caroline usually knows what she wants and how to get it."

"Yes, sir, I believe I'm beginning to understand that. And I thank you for your understanding."

"You're welcome. Just don't mess it up with Caroline. Now, what about this little sick pony over here?" said Raymond as he got up and walked to one of the stalls. "Have to get the vet over here tomorrow, I suspect."

# Chapter 24

Lucas bolted straight up in bed. The scenario had come back to him. The picture at the Jewish Museum. The man. Dada. A younger him. His brother. Of course. The Gestapo. The Gralla family......names probably on the wall....the Wiesenthal Center report said they were there. Could André have seen it?

Lucas looked at the illuminated dial of his watch on the side table. 3:15. His thoughts drifted to the Weber letter. People throwing people out of castle windows. Castle windows.

The thought came to him. Was there a connection? The island. Grandfather. His place....like a castle on top of the hill. Could he be thinking of it? No. Impossible. No. Yet, could something be happening? This is crazy..... Middle of the night - Monday morning in Italy. Lucas could not get back to sleep. By 5 AM, he was up, at the kitchen table and reading his way through one of the newspapers of the previous week he found in the apartment to pass the time.   Caroline found her way to the kitchen a half-hour later, looking groggily at Lucas. "What's up? It's really early."

"Time zones. Body clock still out of synch." He got up, went over to Caroline standing in her t-shirt in the doorway, put his arms around her and kissed her on the top of her forehead. "Slept well, just the same, but need to make a couple of early calls back home. Need to know what my Dada is up to."

Caroline went back to bed saying something about the need for another hour of sleep "before my guy comes back so I can make love to him."

Lucas called the villa. No answer. No recording either. Erik Brandt had not gotten technologically that far as yet.

Lucas then placed a call to his uncle Richard in Munich.

Richard's direct office line rang. *"Ja. Brandt ist hier."* Lucas recognized his uncle's distinctive growly voice.

"Uncle Richard, this is Lucas. I am calling you from America. I have been here for a few days, clearing up things before starting work in Vienna and visiting friends. I trust you are well. We have not spoken since Singapore, but I am doing well, as you probably know through my mum."

"Yes, Lucas, I have heard. Good for you. Must be important, calling from America. Very early over there."

"Yes, it is, but I am concerned about grandfather. It's the reason for my call. I have tried to reach him over the last few days. There has been no answer. Have you spoken with him recently?"

"No, I have not, Lucas. I tried to reach him the other day, just to know how he was doing, but like you, I received no answer. Is there something you are worried about? You sound concerned."

"I am. I have learned some things about Claudia's husband that cause me concern. You must know that grandfather and he do not get along. I am aware of things that are worrisome, quite frankly. I have decided to fly from here to Rome as soon as I can, probably tomorrow, rent a car and go to the island. Could I ask you something?"

"Yes, of course. What is it?"

"Over the next few hours, could you try to find out the whereabouts of Claudia's husband? Of Claudia as well? I don't have her number in Marseille. I was hoping you could help me with that."

"Why, yes, of course. Karl stays in touch with Claudia. He would easily find out, if I can't. Leave it to me. You merely want to know the whereabouts of André, as I understand it. Is that correct?"

"Yes, however, I do not want to raise concerns that may not be warranted. This may all be a false alarm in my head. Just the same, I have concerns that something is up."

"Lucas, Karl and I are aware that Claudia and her husband have not been pleased with your grandfather's plans for disposition of the family property. André's business dealings have always been suspect. They have been in some degree of financial difficulty on and off over the years. I do not know what their situation is at present, but I would be surprised if they would be doing something drastic. Is that what you are suggesting?"

"Maybe. I just don't know at this point. But I need to find out. Could we speak later? I will call you again in a few hours. Is that all right?"

"Yes, let me try to reach Claudia. I will be discreet, but nevertheless see what I can find out. Call me on my mobile at 18:00 hours, Munich time. Here is the number...I should have some news by then. *Auf Wiedersehen.*"

"*Auf Wiedersehen,* Richard."

Later that morning Lucas told Caroline he was changing his travel plans.

"C, I'm not going to go to London after all, unless I can reach my grandfather today. I'm flying to Rome instead and driving to his place. Something is up. I know it. I will be speaking to my uncle Richard at noon, but I have changed my flight plans."

"What could be up?" asked Caroline. "Something happening with your grandfather? A health issue?"

"He lives alone. He's 82. Incommunicado for days now. Has me worried." He would maybe tell Caroline of the André and Claudia issue eventually, but not ow. He had also made the promise to his grandfather.

---

236

Richard Brandt's mobile rang a little after 6 PM in Munich. "Lucas, I managed to reach Karl. He believed Claudia was at her home in Marseille, but would check. He said he had something to ask of Claudia anyway and would call her. He called me an hour ago to say that she was in Marseille, had just returned from a weekend with friends as André was on a business trip to Rome for a few days. André has been away since Friday."

This is troubling, thought Lucas. "So, André is not around, we can't reach Dada. Giuseppe the cobbler across the square hasn't seen him or his jeep for three days. Richard, I have a nagging thought that something is happening on the island. I may be all wrong, but I am going there. I will be flying to New York in a few hours, then on to Rome. I arrive there tomorrow at 3 PM, the earliest I can get there. I will hire a car and drive to Orbatello, then ferry over to the island."

"I will join you. I sense your concern. I haven't seen my father in months, in any case. Not since Singapore. I have a light day tomorrow and Wednesday, as it happens. Let's meet at the Lufthansa departures level at the Rome airport at 4 tomorrow unless I call you. I have your mobile number. See you tomorrow. We'll see what's going on. Hopefully, nothing, but I will be glad to see my father anyway."

# Chapter 25

**The island villa, Sunday night October 17**

Erik had returned in the evening after securing his boat at the marina. It had been a refreshing four days on the water, in and around Orbatello just off the mainland, with a bit of fishing and a lot of reading while anchored in the lovely sheltered coves of the island. The square was quiet. He put the vehicle down around the back of the villa in its usual place, behind the locked gate and secured from view. He entered his little castle on the hill from the back entrance, put away his gear, took a bath to wash off the salt water residue and sun screen from the day on the water, and went to bed.

The knock on the door came just after midnight. Erik was a light sleeper and heard it. A second knock came as he rose, put on his bathrobe and found his way to the main door downstairs. "Ja! Coming," he said in German. "Who is it?" he said before opening the door. "André Gralla, sir. Your son-in-law. Could you please open the door?" quietly replied the man.

Erik opened the door and André entered, walking quickly past the older man clearly surprised at this unexpected visit. "I took the last ferry. I have something to discuss with you." He walked to the table in the center of the room while Erik closed the door.

"You have something to discuss? At this hour?"

"Yes, and now is as good a time as any, despite the hour," replied André.

"The last time you were here, monsieur, it was not pleasant. Will this be more of the same?" Erik said as he turned and approached his surprise visitor who was clearly agitated. Before André could respond, he gestured the visitor toward a chair "Now that you are here, please sit down. Can I offer you something? A glass of wine?"

Ignoring the offer of the chair and the wine, André came around the table and sat on its edge. "I have problems with you, Herr Brandt....Herr Bendt, actually, is it not?"

"This is late, André. Where is Claudia? She's not with you?" Erik clearly recognized the reference to his real name, but gave no indication it surprised him.

"No, she is not. This is between you and me, Herr Bendt." André looked across the table at the distinguished former diplomat who gazed right back into the eyes of his son-in-law.

"So, you know. Yes...Bendt. It was Bendt, but it is no longer and has not been for some time. What does it mean to you? What do you have to say about it?" What is he up to? he asked himself. "What are the problems you refer to? If it is about Claudia's inheritance, that is resolved and it deals with her, not you." Erik was not sure at all where this discussion was going to go, but he could see that the man who just showed up at his island villa, far from his own home, was going to be difficult. This could be an ugly encounter, he thought. It was beginning to be just that.

"No, sir, it is not resolved. I have a proposal for you in that regard, but first, there is something else.......Your brother liquidated my family. You must know that if you don't know it already." Erik flinched, then realized where this was going. "Yes, Erik, Erik Bendt, I am Jewish. My family was Czech Jewish. Prosperous, even wealthy, you would say. They disappeared in 1941. My father who had left for France before the war was the only one who survived. All of the others, gone. My father's brothers and sisters, his father and mother and her own parents - all gone. I have a problem with you because of it. Your brother, your twin brother, actually - you look remarkably alike, by the way, was in charge of the Gestapo in Prague. Have you ever been to the Jewish Museum in Prague, Herr Bendt?" André was rambling, but he could not stop. "No, I guess you haven't. Because you probably know what's there. 77,000 names on the walls. Liquidated. By the Gestapo. There is a picture of someone in a glass case there – a picture of your brother. I swore it was you when I saw it. The Butcher of Prague, head of the Gestapo in Bohemia during the war - Helmut Bendt, your twin brother. I couldn't believe it. The brother of my own father-in-law, who by the way, was cheating my wife of what she should rightly have, who neglected her all her life."

"It was a long time ago, André. I was disgusted with my brother. My father was disgusted with him as well. He disowned him. I never spoke to my brother after a last meeting in 1937. I was ashamed of what a Bendt had become. I changed my name to that of my mother's maiden name. I am sorry, André. I can't bring your family back. This is the legacy for many Germans of my generation, you must know. It is something we can't erase. I am sorry."

"It is not good enough, Erik. An apology is not good enough. I seek retribution. Do you know what my condition would be today if my grandfather had lived, if his business had remained in his hands, what life my own father would have had? Far different than it has been. I myself would have uncles and aunts and cousins, most probably be part of a respected well-to-do family of professionals and businessmen. But I have no Gralla family to know, to be part of. You Germans ruined everything, and your own brother was in charge of much of it." André went on, not letting Erik interject. "I have a recurring nightmare of seeing my grandparents, Maurice and Hanna Gralla, lined up in front of a cattle car, disrobing in a windowless room, collapsing in grotesque death-throws as gas fills the air, then being piled up naked onto carts to be dumped into an open pit on top of hundreds of other naked dead Jews and gypsies and other people the Germans were determined to eradicate from this world. I have this dream quite often. It is very real for me. I may never exorcise myself of it."

"Here is something you may find interesting, monsieur Bendt, and most probably disturbing for someone so devoted as you to preserving his reputation." André had brought with him a small document case. He opened it up, withdrew a piece of paper and placed it on the table. It was a photocopy of a 1948 Vienna newspaper article about Helmut Bendt, the head of the Gestapo in Prague, who was the son of a respected German diplomat before and during the First World War, and who disappeared during the last year of the war after ordering tens of thousands of Czech Jews to their deaths between 1941 and 1944. It was written in German, but André read it out to Erik in French. "There is something else here, Herr Bendt." André brought out a second document which was a copy of Erik's official notification of his name change of 1937.

How did he get this? Swiss records are difficult to obtain. "What do you want, André? What do you propose? This retribution, as you say, what do you want? Money, I suppose?"

"There is something else, Herr Bendt. Something you have kept secret that Claudia has only discovered recently. You are not her real father. Your wife was unfaithful. She had a liking for a young man once and had his child. It was Claudia. I know all of this. I know the whole story."

"Wait a minute. I don't like where you are going with this. Be careful, *monsieur Gralla*." Erik was getting angry.

"You can not like this all you want, sir, but I don't feel like being particularly careful with this information. I don't believe you would be happy if your family knew this, would you? I know all about it. You were not her father. You never loved her. You preferred your sons. You treated them well, but Claudia, not so. You condemned Claudia to living in the little hell of life with her unhappy and reclusive mother who came to hate you. Claudia came to hate you, as well. So, there will be retribution for more than one reason. For me, and for Claudia."

"There are copies of these documents in the possession of people who I merely have to give the word to bring to the attention of the media - I can see it very well, 'the brother of the distinguished German diplomat, Erik Brandt, was responsible for the liquidation of thousands of Jews during the war.' Not nice, *n'est-ce pas?* Certainly not for your sons and their children. Not for your legacy that you cultivated so carefully, to the detriment of the happiness of your own wife and daughter."

"But, there is a simple way to prevent all this. It is to will to Claudia this property, as a gesture to the only surviving female of the family, your only daughter. The proceeds of the sale of the other properties could be divided among your sons. This one, however, would go solely to Claudia. If you do not agree to this, I will have this information put into the public domain. That you are the twin brother of the Butcher of Prague, that your real name is Bendt, not Brandt, that your daughter is the daughter of the nephew of your best friend from university and most damaging to your family legacy, that your wife had a child with another man."

"This is blackmail, Gralla."

"Yes, it is. Call it what you want. Claudia has tried to reason with you, to ask for fair consideration, given your treatment of her and her mother over the years. You have refused."

"Is she aware of what you are doing?"

"No, she is not. She has given up on this with you. I am doing this on her behalf. She has been deceived all her life. Her mother never told her the truth of her parentage. You neglected her. She was miserable until she met me. I am doing this for her. She tried with you. She got nowhere. Time to settle the score. *Régler les comptes, monsieur Bendt.*"

"This is mostly for you, André. Let's be honest. I know of your financial dealings, your underhanded ways of doing business. No banks will deal with you anymore. You must be desperate to do something like this. What does Claudia know of what you have told me?"

"She knows about her real father. She found your wife's diary after her death. Read all about it. About my family, she knows nothing. She doesn't have to. You and I are going to make sure of that with this deal. In any case, Herr Bendt, I am here. I have presented you the deal. What will it be?"

"With you alone here, there is no deal. I may do something for Claudia. I want to see her here. This is despicable, Gralla." Erik was in a bind. He knew it. Gralla had all the cards. He would have to hold out, find a way to call his bluff. He was not going to give this property away to this craven, ignoble man, but had to find a way to prevent him from carrying out his threat. "You know, Gralla, that blackmail is a crime in Italy and in France. This is extortion."

"Claudia is not coming. This is between you and I. Call it what you want. But we are going to do it."

"Gralla, I can't undo what my brother did. He was a monster. I regret that your family was a part of that. It is a stain on the German people, a stain that will be there forever. I am sorry for that, truly sorry. It has been particularly difficult for me. But, you will not blackmail me. I will not submit to it. Like I said, I will do something for Claudia, but I will not take this property away from the whole family to turn it over to you to do with as you wish. I am certain the property will not stay long in the hands of Claudia if I accept to do it. I won't."

Erik continued after a pause, probing André to see how far he was prepared to go. "I won't live forever. Claudia will have her share of the monies from the sales of the other properties. Is that not enough for you? Do you need the money so desperately that you cannot wait? The proceeds from that will be significant. Why this desperation? Is your financial situation that bad that you would precipitate all of this?"

"Herr Bendt, you will do as I say. I have the text of the will that you sent to your offspring last year. I have drawn up a letter for you to sign which will be delivered to your lawyer in Bonn instructing him to change the will, to have this property offered for sale with the proceeds from the sale to revert to Claudia, as your only daughter, with the proceeds of the other properties to revert to your sons as they are disposed of. You will be able to live in any of those other properties you have. Why not St-Remy? It is in the south of France. Not such a bad place to live - no stairs to walk up for an old man. And if you ever break this agreement or speak of it while you are living, I can assure you, I will release all of this to whomever I please."

"This is preposterous, Gralla. You are going to leave. Now. I won't hear any more from you."

"I think not, sir. You are going to sign that letter and the change to your will."

"I refuse. Never."

"I told you what I would do. The story of your family, and the story of your wife. Will not be nice."

"Out, Gralla! Out!"

*Time to go to Plan B*, André said to himself under his breath. He had hoped to avoid the nastiness of what he was about to put into motion, but the old man had left him no choice.

He went around the table, grabbed Erik Brandt's arms, brought them behind the straight-backed chair, took out the length of rope and tied the old man's hands behind his back.

Erik did his best to resist but the younger man was far stronger than he. "Gralla, you loathsome rat....." was all that the old man managed to cry out before André stuffed a cloth into his mouth and secured it with a length of fabric tied behind his head.

"Herr Brandt, you had the chance to change your mind. Sorry about this," whispered André into the ear of the struggling elderly man on the teetering chair. He then took the needle out of his pocket, put the tip of it in the small vial and pricked Erik's shoulder. The old man went limp within seconds.

André placed the call from his mobile.

"This is Gralla. We put the plan in motion. You are to arrive here after dark and go to the village in the center of the island. You have the plan of the island and of the villa. There is a secret entrance down around the back below the wall overlooking the cliff. No one will see you enter. The old man will be in his bed, sedated. An untraceable solution with a two-day effect. When there is no one on the square, carry out the task. Take the documents that are under the old man's pillow and leave them on the table before the double window on the third floor overlooking the square, with the suicide note on top. When the deed has been done, take a picture of the square below with the night vision camera that I have left under the pillow. Meet me in Rome at this address on Wednesday with the camera and I will have the 50,000 Euros for you. To be sure, do not leave any finger-prints. This must appear as a suicide."

The man at the other end of the line recognized that the plan was as agreed the week before. "Understood. See you Wednesday afternoon." Click.

André had mused to himself. Defenestration. The Bohemian way. I am a Bohemian after all - a Bohemian Jew, yes, but Bohemian just the same. André had realized something else about this tradition. None of the perpetrators of the known defenestrations in Bohemian history were ever prosecuted or punished for their deed. Prague in 1420 and 1618, Ronsperg in 1862, and the incident with Masaryk after the war. This defenestration will not break that tradition, he thought. It won't even be viewed as a defenestration. For everyone, it will be a suicide. Marco had found these guys. Part of the plan to get repaid by his errant cousin. André met them two weeks before in a cafe in Navaro. Calabrians. Did much of Marco and Luca Scalia's dirty work. Very good at what they did. They would ensure that Erik Brandt was dead by the time he fell to the square below. Broken neck. 25,000 Euros upon agreement. 50,000 Euros upon completion of the deed, if required, which it now was. Upon André's command, the men would arrive by power boat after dark, walk up to the villa, enter from the back, carry out the murder, then return to the boat and to the marina outside Rome. The letter to the lawyer had been drawn up in German with a faked Erik signature, using as model the signature on the original copy of the will he had found in Claudia's papers. Marco helped with the forgery. The letter made reference to his remorse for not being a better father to Claudia, the deception of his true identity and the difficult life he had their mother endure while he was spending his career ensuring the honor of the family name. A different letter in German that Marco's German speaking contact typed out and provided to André would also be left on the table next to the other documents and the old newspaper article. It was a letter from an anonymous source in Vienna describing Erik's relationship with the Butcher of Prague. It presented the author as a descendant of Prague Jews killed in the Holocaust and said that the information would soon be provided to Der Spiegel magazine and other German-language media.

André would be in Rome when the time of death would be established, with a solid alibi. He had made sure no one saw him arrive at the villa. Nobody on the street, no lights on around the square. The killers would leave no trace. They were professionals. The family would be distressed at Erik's suicide. The note would tell all, though, and hopefully the family would not contest the revised will. The newspaper article and the revelation of the identity of their father's brother would be devastating, explaining the suicide, but the revised will, under German law, should prevail. André counted upon the sympathy of Karl and Richard for their sister and resign themselves to the revised disposition of the properties. The brother in South America would maybe object, but be in the minority if he chose to do so. Not much to worry about there, based on the man's behavior over the years. Claudia would soon enough be encouraged to sell the villa in the months ahead as the taxes and upkeep would be prohibitive. She knew no one on the island and it would be far from his own business. Impractical to live there, despite its cachet and attractiveness. They would buy another home near Nice or Cannes with part of the proceeds and André would pay off all his debts. Claudia would never know about his grandparents, their disappearance at the hands of Erik's brother. There would be no evident connection between André Gralla and the death of Erik Brandt. Marco had accepted the plan as a way to get repaid, at the cost of an old German's life. He and his family had never liked Germans in the first place. The war had left its traces in Italy as well as elsewhere.

At 5 AM, after carrying the sedated Erik Brandt to his bed and placing the documents and the camera under the pillow, André retrieved the Fiat with the false registration that Marco had provided him in Orbatello that was parked down the hill. He made it to the dock for the 6 AM ferry to the mainland. He left the Fiat where he had found it in Orbatello, got into the Peugeot parked three blocks away and easily made it to his 2 PM meeting in Rome.

**Tuesday, 8 PM**

The two men tethered the boat to the dock at the far end of the Porto marina, and then walked up the hill, discreetly avoiding the road in the darkness, to the village and the castle-like villa in the Casamatta quarter of town. By 9:00 PM, they had found the hidden back entrance close to the cliff behind the village, per

André's instructions, and entered the lower level of the four story structure, passing through the wine cellar to a winding stairway to the street level.

At 9 PM, the last ferry of the day from Orbatello arrived at the main dock of Giglio Porto. The Opel sedan rented at the Rome Airport made its way up the winding hill to the village. Lucas had managed to reach Giuseppe from Orbatello before embarking, agreeing to meet on the square as soon as they could get there from the ferry dock.

Giuseppe was agitated as he ran to the car as it arrived. "Lucas, look over there. The windows above the square are open. Your grandfather would never have those windows open at this time of night. I heard voices from the villa not more than five minutes ago. No lights are on. Very strange."

My uncle Richard is with me. Richard nodded to Giuseppe as he got out of the car and looked up at the third-floor window, then addressed the old man. *"Buona sera, signore.* It has been a long time."

Lucas interjected before Giuseppe could respond. "Have you seen him today?"

"No, I have not seen him. Not today. I haven't seen him since last week," responded the old man.

Lucas looked up. The double caisson window was open. Defenestration. It's going to happen. "Giuseppe, you need to call the *caribinieri* Now. Have them come here. Tell them a robbery or maybe worse, could very well be about to take place." Richard grabbed Lucas' arm and motioned him to the door. It was locked. Lucas called out to Giuseppe who was about to enter his shop. "Giuseppe, do you not have a key to the place? I think I gave you one when I was here, so you could find it?"

"*Si*, you did give me one. I have it in the shop. I will call the caribinieri as well." Giuseppe emerged a few seconds later, hurried across the square and gave Lucas the key.

The two men in the back of the house two stories above, in Erik Brandt's bedroom, were at that moment hoisting the old man to bring him to the study on the other side of the villa in front of the open windows. They had heard nothing of the arrival of the car below and the ensuing discussion. The men had been careful to wipe clean everything they had touched in the house. They had placed the documents André had left under the man's pillow on the table in the study and had returned to the bedroom to fetch the old man.

Lucas and Richard entered the ground floor hall, making as little noise as possible. "Sssshhh. Footsteps above. Do we go upstairs?" whispered Lucas to his uncle.

"We had better. Something is happening, I'm afraid," replied his uncle as they huddled before going further. They crossed the hall on their tip toes and walked slowly up the stairway. The police better be on their way, thought Lucas.

The man carrying Erik stopped in his tracks and whispered to his colleague. "Someone is here. In the house. I just heard something from over there." He put Erik down. The other man, who had drawn the task of breaking the old man's neck - the other would throw him out the window - crossed to the other side of the room and placed himself behind the corner leading to the stairway. He listened for footsteps as he drew the revolver from his jacket.

Lucas and Richard slowly made their way up the stairway to the third floor. The man nearest them in the darkness was ready to slam the first person entering the study on the head with the barrel of the revolver, when he heard the faint siren of the police car coming up the hill. The distraction was enough for Lucas to notice the shadow of a figure to his right. He rushed the man, tackling him rugby style from his days on the pitch. The gun fell from the man's hand. Lucas managed to punch him before being punched himself. The other man lunged at Richard and threw him to the floor. At that moment, the police car with the siren blaring entered the square. The two hit men who were seconds away from disposing of the elderly Erik Brandt ran down the stairs to the wine cellar and found their way out the back entrance. The two policemen entered and went up the stairs. By this time, Lucas had turned the lights on and with Richard, had gone to the aid of his grandfather. He felt his pulse and saw that he was breathing. Richard cradled the head of his father. "Thank God. We got here in time. Lucas, you were right. These were killers. It was going to happen." Richard then turned to the *carabinieri*, and through Giuseppe who translated, informed them of what had transpired. One of the officers took out his radiophone and spoke to a colleague in the village. Richard could make out from what he was saying that two potential killers were on the loose on the island and that the port villages needed to be covered.  A man was nearly thrown to his death from the third floor of his home to the square below. A villa on Casamatta Square. Family members arrived in time to interrupt the operation - suspects escaped - we believe they are on foot - no description available.

The two assailants managed to reach their boat in the darkness of the unlighted marina at the end of the dock at Porto. They made their way out to sea and a return to the port near Rome and their car. The operation had failed. Someone found out about it. Marco will not be happy. We will see about the money. Nobody was supposed to know about this.

Within an hour, a detective from the island police force was at the villa, interviewing Lucas, Richard and Giuseppe while a doctor was tending to Erik. An ambulance arrived and the elderly man was taken to the island hospital. The doctor informed Richard and Lucas that Erik was probably not in danger of dying from what he had been given, but that he should be looked at in intensive care, just the same. By that time, Richard and Lucas had retrieved and read the documents left on the table in the study. Only later after Erik gained consciousness and unveiled what had happened did they understand that the perpetrator of it all truly was André Gralla.

The hit man reached the special number of Marco Scalia. It was late. There was no answer. The voicemail prompt came on. "Marco, somebody knew about this. Two men arrived at the same time we did. Could not have been a coincidence. We could not complete the mission. We had to run. The police were on their way. The old man is probably still alive. You had better get in touch with that guy, André, and work something out. Nobody was supposed to know about this. We are out 50,000 Euros. Not happy about this. Not going to speak with him until we talk. Over to you."

Meanwhile, André tried reaching the hit men. There was no answer. He tried every fifteen minutes. Something has gone wrong. No reason why they would not answer if the mission had gone as planned. He was desperate to find out what had happened. He could not sleep. He went out for a walk. Middle of the night. No news. This is bad. What could have gone wrong? These guys are pros.

A little after 6AM, André got his answer. It was Marco. The operation had failed. Somebody had shown up at the same time. "Who did you tell about this, André? Could not have been a coincidence."

André was incredulous. He could not believe what he was hearing. The whole plan had failed. Documents in the villa. Erik still alive. Everything I said to him. The blackmail. Everything. It's all there for the family to see. The police. Erik will certainly tell them it was me. People will be looking for me. The thoughts raced through his head as he tried to find something to say to his cousin, whose next question André knew, would be how he was now going to cover what he owed him.

"I can't believe this. Marco, I swear. I spoke to no one about this. No one. I covered my tracks. No one saw me. I am sure."

"Well, my dear cousin, you are in deep shit. You better have an alternate plan. And quickly. I will call you later. I need to see you. The guys expect to be paid. First things first. You need to have the 50,000 Euros as a first step. Tomorrow in Genoa. I don't care what plans you have. You need to change them." Click.

Lucas and Richard were in the hospital room when Erik awoke. He turned his head and recognized them. "André. Tied me up. Where am I?" as he looked around.

Richard answered. "Father, you are in the hospital on the island. You were drugged. Some men tried to kill you. You are going to be all right, though."

"André. What he did to me. Threatened me. Blackmail. Things about my past."

"Yes. Looks like he had a plan. We can talk about all this when you feel better. Lucas figured it out. Suspected André was up to something. We got here in time. But you are going to be fine."

With that, Erik slipped back into unconsciousness before he could respond. Lucas and Richard would stay with him through the day until he had fully regained consciousness, at which time he would be told of what had happened.

Richard placed the call to his sister in Marseille. "Claudia, your father is in the hospital on the island. I think you should come."

"What happened? Is he all right? Is he dying?" asked Claudia at the other end.

"No, he is not dying. But somebody tried to kill him. I think you should come."

"André has the car. He is in Rome. I will call him, but if I am to go, I will have to find another car."

"I would not talk to André just yet, Claudia. Come here first."

"What do you mean, not talk to André? What is going on? Is he involved somehow? Why do I have to be there, and before I talk to my husband?"

"Claudia, believe me. You should come here and as soon as possible. You will understand everything when you get here."

"All right. I will rent a car. I should arrive early evening if all goes well."

"Let us know when you expect to arrive. The last ferry is at 8 PM."

## Friday, October 22

André Gralla arrived in Panama City through Rio de Janeiro, then Quito, Ecuador, using a fake Italian passport he had made up some years before, hoping to leave no trace of his ultimate whereabouts. He had 80,000 Euros in his baggage. It would have to last. It was all the cash he could bring together in the day he had to wrap up his affairs. He did not meet with Marco. He did not speak with his wife. He just left.

Claudia Gralla arrived on the island. Karl was there as well after being told of what had happened. Richard received his sister at the villa and with Lucas and Karl present, explained to her what had happened.

"Claudia, this is not going to be pleasant. André, your husband, very nearly succeeded in having our father murdered. Thrown out of the window here to the cobblestones below by hired assassins and making it look like a suicide. I am sorry to have to tell you this, but I am afraid it is true. The evidence is all here. When Dada woke up this afternoon, he told us everything. André was threatening to blackmail him unless he turned this villa over to you. Immediately. He had drawn up forged documents - a letter to the lawyer in Bonn, a revised will. He had also produced a threatening letter from someone in Vienna, probably forged as well, about the activities of our father's brother during the war. Something we did not know about. Not nice reading. I understand why our father never told us about that. André had somehow discovered it."

Claudia broke into tears. Her head fell into her hands. "What was he going to blackmail father with?" she asked.

"He threatened to make public the connection of Dada to the organizer of massacres of Jews in Czechoslovakia during the war. He produced a copy of an article from a newspaper in Vienna in 1948 about the man, who was head of the Gestapo in Prague. It was his brother. Something we did not know about, that he had kept secret from us all our lives. And, about your mother. Your birth."

"My birth? I know about my birth. My real father is someone else. It is time you know that. I learned of it last year with the discovery of Mother's diary. André was going to blackmail him with that as well?"

"With the honor of our mother. That she had an affair, that she was unfaithful. Father was protective of our mother's reputation. He told us this afternoon that he did everything to conceal the true story of your parentage, as it would impinge on Mother's honor. He regretted how it all turned out, the estrangement, the difficult relationship with you. Sorry for everything. Let's go to the hospital. Father wants to see you."

Claudia entered the room first. "Hello, father."

"I am sorry, Claudia, for everything I have put you through. I was not a good father to you. You deserved better."

Claudia approached the bed where her father lay, bent over and put her arms around the old man. "I'm sorry too, Daddy."

"I'm not your real daddy, you know that, my dear," Erik replied as his daughter maintained her embrace. "It was kept from you. It had to be that way."

"I know that. Mama never let on."

"She couldn't, Claudia. It would have been devastating for you, and I must say, selfishly, for me as well. I am sorry we were not better parents for you. Can you forgive me?"

Claudia realized at that moment that her father, her adopted father as it were, was all she had left. She also realized that what she had always wanted when she was little - the love of her father, could be found after all. It was right in front of her.

"Daddy, I'm sorry too. You are my only father and always have been. I love you." She took his hand, bent over and kissed him on the forehead. "I won't leave you."

"And I will not abandon you, Claudia. Never again."

After a moment in the room where everybody present had a smile on their face with a tear or two in their eyes, Erik asked the question. "Can anybody tell me what happened to André? Does anybody where he is? Is this over? Do I have to worry about him?"

Richard, the lawyer in the family, answered. "We don't know. The police are looking for him. I have hired security for the villa until we know more." Everyone looked at Claudia.

"I don't know. I have tried to reach him for two days. He is not answering. I don't know." She broke down in tears. "I don't know..tried to kill you....money, his damn need for money..I don't know...."

Claudia knew it was over. She could never go back to him, even be around him. It was over. She rose, turned and embraced Karl, the nearest Brandt in the room.

# Chapter 26

Claudia Brandt never heard from her husband again. By the middle of December, she had come to live with her father on the island. Erik had insisted upon it. Claudia accepted. It was not just about money, as she had none - André had taken all that there was. She wanted to. She would look after her father and start anew. In May, Claudia opened a boutique of women's and children's clothing in Giglio Porto just off the waterfront and down from the quay where the luxury cruise liners docked. Erik paid for the initial inventory and set-up costs. The shop did well right from the start.

Within a few months, Claudia had been invited to dinner by different young men on the island. One of them, Francisco Bellacolli was a lawyer from Siena and had opened a law office on the island the year before. Claudia had been to dinner with him a few times and they spent time that summer on her father's boat sailing around the bays and coves of the island.

By the summer of 2008, Claudia and Francisco had been married close to seven years, were very much in love and were the proud parents of two energetic little boys who loved to play in the square in front of the villa they all shared with Claudia's father.

Lucas Brandt welcomed Caroline to Vienna for the U.S. Thanksgiving weekend that November of 1999. By the following summer, Caroline was working in Vienna for the United Nations. in an office not far from the cafe where she and her handsome Englishman had met the summer before. She could not know, nor could Lucas, that it was the same Viennese cafe where Lucas' grandmother was courted by the true father of his aunt Claudia in another time.

In August, Raymond and Lorraine Weber visited their daughter in Vienna, where Raymond's great-grandfather had toiled before coming to America. They traveled to Prague and visited the various castle towns on the way through the country, themselves connecting with the heritage of the family's Bohemian past.

By the summer of 2008, Lucas Brandt Development Associates had been operating for four years with a growing staff based in London and consulting contracts from many international organizations around the world. Caroline Weber Brandt was the firm's Vice-President of Research. She had piloted the firm's acquisition of Mid-America Research Group of Kansas City the year before, subsequently turning that firm's focus away from the supporting of conservative points of view to non-partisan public affairs research for international clients. She managed to see her parents every few months to tell them all about the activities of their two grandchildren growing up in London and learning to play football the English way.

A few years before, Raymond Weber had received permission from the Bishop of Kansas City and eventually the parish priests of all of the original twelve Bohemian Catholic churches of Kansas to install plaques in prominent places near the entrances of the churches with the inscription:

**Built with the support of Thomas**
**Weber, a devoted Bohemian and**
**Catholic, in the year 189_.**

St. Joseph's Church in the fields of the vanished village of Flush had the biggest stone monument carrying that inscription of all, a four foot high slab of sculpted sandstone on the little square in front of the church with the plaque sitting prominently on top. In the summer of 2002, St. Joe's had reopened for regular Mass every Sunday with Father Francis Kurtz presiding. It had been awhile since anyone had noticed weeds protruding between the concrete sections of the pavement out front. People said it felt good not having to go to Sunday Mass in Wamego anymore.

Erik Brandt lived another ten years, helping his daughter re-start her life, enjoying the young family she was raising, receiving his sons and their families for holidays on the island, and spending many of his days on his boat fishing and playing cards with his old friend Giuseppe, who had finally closed his shop and retired. The close relationship with his grandson, Lucas, solidified forever through their saving of each other's lives in that year of 1999, was there for everyone in the family to see in the old man's twilight years. One day, Erik's heart simply stopped working. As the darkness came, he managed to have a last thought of a life redeemed.

Before the family had left the island that October of 1999, Karl asked Lucas how he had come to suspect something was going to happen to his grandfather.

"The Bohemian Connection. It's a long story."

# Author's Notes

All of the places mentioned in this novel exist and most of the historical incidents described actually occurred, although some have been fictionalized. The characters in the novel are fictional, although some have been based on people I have known. I explain below.

The Defenestration of 1618 at the Castle of Prague actually occurred. It triggered the bloody Thirty Years' War of Europe. Count Vilem Slavata existed, was one of the three people thrown out the window that day, and lived to be named by the Habsburg Emperor a few years later as Chancellor of Bohemia. Count Slavata's willing of an estate at Ronsperg to his rescuer and that man's lineage to a Cobourg-Strauss family is fiction.

Other defenestrations have taken place in what is now the Czech Republic. The first one, in 1419, was religiously provoked as well, having to do with the fallout of the execution of Jan Hus, the rebel priest. On that day in 1419, an angry mob of Hussite peasant rebels stormed the town hall on Charles Square in Prague and threw the judge, the mayor and several city council members out the window. They all either died in the fall or were slain by the crowd outside. Another happened on 24 September 1483, when a violent overthrow of the municipal governments of the Old and New Towns ended with throwing the Old Town Reeve and the bodies of seven slain aldermen out the windows of the respective town halls. Defenestration has been used to describe the death of Jan Masaryk, the popular wartime leader of the Czech government in exile who was found below the bathroom window of the building of the Czechoslovak Ministry of Foreign Affairs on 10 March 1948. The official report listed the death as a suicide, but there have been persistent rumors that he was murdered, either by the nascent Communist government in which he served as Foreign Minister, or by the Soviet secret services.

Another occurred in Prague in 1848 during a popular uprising but I have not succeeded in discovering any of the details of such.

The actual owners of the Ronsperg estate and castle for over two hundred years until 1948 were the Coudonhove-Kalergi family. That family is one of the most distinguished of Austria and pre-war Bohemia. The last owner of the castle from that family was Richard von Coudonhove-Kalergi, the son of Count Heinrich of the same name, and his Japanese wife, who he married when he was Ambassador of Austria to Japan. The countess was the first Japanese national to ever marry a Westerner. There was no defenestration at that castle in 1862 or at any other time, as far as I know, and the Cobourg-Strauss family in the novel is one of fiction. The castle in the center of the village of Pobezovice, with the former name of Ronsperg, after being left to deteriorate after the Second World War, is currently under renovation. My wife and I toured the grounds of the castle in September 2012.

Westmoreland, Kansas is a town of 790 people (as of 2011) and the seat of Pottawatomie County in north-central Kansas. The site of the former village of Flush is approximately five miles southwest of Westmoreland. St. Joseph's Church of Flush still stands today with weekly Masses served by the visiting priest from Wamego. The cemetery across the road, surrounded by fields of wheat and corn, contains the remains of a number of Webers and other Bohemian, Austrian and German immigrants. The rectory exists as well. I do not really know what it contains. The Weber family in the novel is fictional, but based on the story of a real one of another name that came to Kansas from Bohemia.

There are many Catholic churches in Kansas that were built by the Bohemian immigrant community. I am not aware of how any of them were financed. The story is fictional in that regard. The Jesuit Seminary of St. Marys is real. St.Marys is fifteen miles east of Wamego on Kansas Highway 24. It was one of the first Catholic outposts on the plains, founded as an Indian mission in 1848. It is the site of the first Catholic cathedral west of the Missouri River and east of the Rockies. It operates today as a college. The chancellor of Imperial Germany, Otto von Bismarck, did expel the Jesuits from Germany in 1872 and a number of them came to America. It could be that one or more of them found their way to Kansas and St. Marys.

The places in Vienna named in the story exist. The Cafe Griensteidl on Michaelerplatz next to the entrance to the Hofburg Palace is a popular cafe to this day, and the Burgtheatre not far away is one of Vienna's leading theatres. The Palmenhaus im Burggarten restaurant in the extended part of the arboretum structure overlooking Burggarten park behind the Hofburg Palace is an excellent place to have dinner on a summer evening. For thirty years there existed in London a David Black Oriental Carpets in Portland Road. It was the finest carpet shop in London and was owned by a dear friend of mine.

The castle towns of Bohemia described in the story are real, lovely and full of history. The tour of the Jindrichuv Hradec castle and the explanation of the defenestration of its owner in Prague in 1618 formed much of the inspiration for this story.

The Jewish Museum of Prague is real and contains much of what I have described, including the names of the 77,000 Czech Jews deported to their deaths during the Second World War. The Pilsner Urquell brewery in Plzen is worth visiting, particularly its extensive network of underground tunnels dug in the 19th century to provide cool storage in huge barrels for the beer that is produced there. The brewery complex does sit next to the soccer stadium of Plzen FC Victoria football club.

The town of Giglio Castello on the island of Isola del Giglio off the western coast of Italy certainly exists, with a castle that overlooks the delightful small town of narrow streets and alleyways and houses built on the crest of the mountain that dominates the center of that island, and from which one can observe the surrounding Mediterranean in all directions.

T.C.

June 2013

# Other novels by the author